THE
HORSESHOE
TRILOGIES

Sweet Charity

THE HORSESHOE TRILOGIES

Sweet Charity

by
Lucy Daniels

VOLO

HYPERION
New York

Special thanks to Jennie Walters.
Thanks also to Richard Jones M.R.C.V. S., for reviewing the
veterinary material contained in this book.

Text copyright © 1999 by Working Partners Limited
Illustrations copyright © 2002 by Tristan Elwell

First published in England by Hodder Children's Books under the series title
Perfect Ponies.

The Horseshoe Trilogies, Volo, and the Volo colophon are trademarks of
Disney Enterprises, Inc.

Printed in the United States of America

First U.S. edition, 2002
1 3 5 7 9 10 8 6 4 2

This book is set in 12.5-point Life Roman.
ISBN 0-7868-1620-1 (paperback edition)
ISBN 0-7868-1962-6 (hardcover edition)
Visit www.volobooks.com

THE HORSESHOE TRILOGIES

Sweet Charity

CHAPTER ONE

Josie Grace and her horse, Charity, were riding through the woods in the early evening sunshine. There was no one else around, and everything was quiet except for the pounding of the gray mare's hooves as she cantered along the bridle path. They had just turned the corner when suddenly a riderless horse came bolting toward them, causing Josie to scream out in alarm. The horse skidded to a halt and stood, snorting, in the middle of the path, its coat glistening with sweat.

Josie calmed the frightened animal and led him back up the path alongside Charity. She had to try to find his rider, who might have been injured or even be lying unconscious somewhere in the woods.

A few minutes later, after they had only covered a short distance, Josie heard a faint cry from up ahead, and as they came nearer, she saw a young man, lying by the side of the path and clutching his leg. His face was white with pain, but he managed to tell her what had happened. His horse, startled by a rabbit, had reared and thrown him, and he thought his leg might have been broken. If Josie could find his aunt at the nearby riding stables, she would send help.

Josie and Charity galloped off down the path and quickly found the stables. There they saw a frail old lady, struggling to muck out one of the stalls.

No, Josie thought to herself, that doesn't sound right. An old lady wouldn't muck out stalls. What else could she be doing? Ah, yes—this was better: *. . . saw a frail old lady, watering flowers in a beautifully kept front garden . . . .*

She must have had this daydream at least twenty

times. The old lady turned out to be the owner of the stables and was grateful for Josie's help. She would call an ambulance immediately, and then, while they were waiting for it to arrive, would tell Josie about a troubling problem she had. The stables urgently needed a well-trained horse and a qualified instructor to give riding lessons and occupy the vacant house next door. Josie would then tell her what an incredible coincidence this was, because her mother was a riding instructor, and sadly, *they* had to leave the stables where they themselves were currently living.

She had just reached this triumphant moment when her father's voice interrupted her thoughts from the end of the table. "Josie!" he said. "I've asked you to pass the milk three times. Wake up!"

"Oh, sorry," Josie said, coming back down to earth with a bump. "What did you say?"

"The milk, please," Robert Grace said slowly and clearly, and then smiled at her. "For my cornflakes. It's in the pitcher in front of you."

"Oh, right," Josie said, passing it to him.

"Thanks, sweetheart," he said. "You were miles away! What were you thinking about?"

"Oh, just daydreaming," Josie sighed, taking a bite of her toast and jam. It was Saturday morning, and she was sitting in the kitchen with her mom and dad. She sighed again. There were no magical solutions to the problems they were facing. They had to leave School Farm, the place where Josie had lived for all of her twelve years, and she was going to have to part with her very special horse, Charity.

Josie had been over this a hundred times in her head, but there seemed to be no alternative. For fourteen years, the Graces had been renting their house and the riding stables her mother ran from an old lady. Mrs. Wetherall had died suddenly a few months before, leaving the place to her nephew. His lawyers had sent the Graces a letter saying that he would be selling the house and land to a developer; they had three months to close the stables and move out.

Those three months were flying by, and Josie had already said good-bye to the two other horses at Grace's Stables: Faith, the elderly bay mare who'd been there from the very beginning, and Hope, the sweet-natured gray who was Charity's mother. Now they had less than three weeks to find a new home for Charity, as well as for themselves. Josie's mom and dad had explained to her that they just couldn't afford to keep a horse once the riding school had closed.

Josie gave another deep sigh and stared out the kitchen window. The advertisement for Charity would be in the local paper that Wednesday.

"I've got a couple of lessons this morning, and then we're going house-hunting in the afternoon," Mary Grace told her daughter. "You'll come with us, won't you?"

Josie shook her head. "No, thanks," she said, looking down at her plate. "I don't really feel like it. You just find somewhere and tell me when it's all decided." She didn't want to think about living anywhere else until she absolutely had to.

"I wish you would come along," her father said. "I don't like the thought of you here on your own, feeling miserable."

"It's all right, Dad. I won't be on my own," Josie said, seeing his anxious expression. "Anna's coming over after lunch."

Anna Marshall had been Josie's best friend for three years now. She lived a couple of miles away in the village of Northgate with her mother and twin brother, Ben.

"Good! If anyone can cheer you up, it'll be Anna," said Mrs. Grace, starting to clear away the breakfast things. "Something tells me we won't be away too long, anyway. We've only got a couple of houses to see, and I don't think either of them are very good prospects."

"Right. I'm going to bring Charity in from the field and prepare her for the first lesson," Josie said. She put her plate in the sink and headed out of the kitchen with Basil, the family's terrier, scurrying along at her heels. She wanted to spend as much time as possible with her horse while she still had the chance.

"We're not starting until ten today, so there's no need to hurry," Mrs. Grace called after her.

Josie walked down the path from School Farm to the stable yard. Basil gave a playful bark at Millie, one of the Graces' two black-and-white cats, who was sitting outside the tack room, her tail curled neatly around her paws. She glanced away disdainfully and stalked off to join her brother, Rascal, who was playing in the straw in one of the stalls on the other side of the yard.

"Never mind, Basil," Josie said, giving his smooth head a pat. "Maybe there'll be a rabbit for you to chase in the field." She felt under the flowerpot outside the tack-room door for the key to unlock it.

"Hi, Josie," came a soft voice, making Josie nearly jump out of her skin.

She whirled around and saw a young blond-haired girl standing just behind her, smiling rather uncertainly. "Oh, Kirsty!" she said. "You nearly gave me a heart attack. Where did you come from?"

Kirsty Fisher had been coming to the stables for nearly two years. She lived in Northgate, too, so it was easy for her to walk up to the stables. Lately, she'd been spending more and more time there. Charity had always been her favorite horse, and she'd asked if she could continue riding her right up until the Graces sold her. Mrs. Grace was happy to agree—she wanted to give lessons for as long as possible, and she knew how fond Kirsty was of Charity.

"Sorry, Josie. I didn't mean to scare you," Kirsty said, twisting her hands together awkwardly. "I thought I could help you bring Charity in from the field. I've got a lesson later on, but Mom said it would probably be all right if I came up now."

Kirsty had one sister who was much older than she was, and Josie guessed Kirsty was sometimes pretty lonely at home. "Of course you can come with me," Josie said, trying not to feel irritated. She'd really been looking forward to some quiet time alone with Charity. Still, there would be other days. She unlocked the tack-room door, and they went in.

"It looks so bare in here now that there's only Charity's things left," Kirsty said, looking around the whitewashed walls. Besides keeping Hope and Charity, Mrs. Grace had boarded three other horses at the stables that she looked after and helped to exercise. Their owners had recently moved them and all their tack to another yard, and now Grace's Stables seemed very empty.

"I know," Josie replied, unhooking a head collar and scooping up a handful of horse treats from the bag by the door. "Come on, let's go and see what she's up to."

Together they walked back across the yard and past the outdoor schooling ring toward the field.

Charity was grazing in a far corner, swishing her tail to keep away the flies that were settling on her every now and then. Josie noticed Kirsty's pale face light up when she caught sight of the horse. Making a huge effort to be generous, she passed her the head collar. "Here," she said. "Do you want to try catching Charity?"

"Oh, yes, please!" Kirsty answered, obviously delighted.

"Just hide the head collar behind your back and hold out some of these nuts," Josie advised. "I'll give her a call."

Charity had lifted her head when she'd first seen them and now decided to trot over, her mane flowing and the muscles beneath her gray coat rippling as she moved. "She is so beautiful, isn't she?" Kirsty said, as Charity pushed her soft pink muzzle forward to take the tidbit.

Charity's silver-gray coat was speckled with darker hairs, and Josie had always thought "flea-bitten"—which was the proper term—hardly did it justice. She had a paler blaze running down her face, and a pure white mane and tail. Her legs were long and straight, her body was perfectly proportioned, and she carried her head proudly on a gracefully arched neck.

"I love her eyes best of all," Josie said, helping Kirsty buckle up the head collar. "They've got such a sparkle in them. You can tell just by looking at her how much fun she is to ride, even if she does get into mischief."

Josie and her mother had grown used to Charity's little tricks over the years. When she was still only young, she had worked out how to open the bolt on her stall door with her teeth, and was discovered cantering around the yard. Mrs. Grace had to fit another bolt at the bottom of the door after that, to keep the frisky mare out of trouble.

Kirsty took the lead rope and brought Charity carefully back across the field. When they were nearly there, she said to Josie, who was walking alongside, "Charity's not really going to be sold, is she?"

"I'm afraid so," Josie replied, opening the gate. "It's going to be tough with the stables closing."

"I always thought you had loads of money, living here with all your horses," Kirsty said, looking at the fields and paddocks that surrounded School Farm as she led Charity out of the field.

"Well, the horses that board here didn't belong to us, and our horses all had to work for their living," Josie replied. "Besides, Mrs. Wetherall didn't charge much rent because she was just glad to see the stables put to good use. So, we're going to have to pay a whole lot more to live somewhere else."

"But your parents know how much Charity means to you," Kirsty said. "They won't really make you give her up, will they?"

"I don't think they've got much choice," Josie sighed. "Come on, let's start getting her ready for your lesson."

"Thanks for letting me bring her in," Kirsty said, as they walked Charity over to the stalls. "It was great!"

"That's okay," Josie said, slightly ashamed of how annoyed she'd felt when she'd first seen Kirsty. On an impulse, she added, "Look, Mom's told me to clear out some of my old things and I thought I'd do that this afternoon. Do you want to come over? I think there's a pair of riding pants that might fit you."

"Yes, please!" Kirsty said eagerly. "I'd really like that, Josie. Thanks!"

"Great," Josie replied. Then she remembered, too late, that Anna was coming over, too, and Kirsty really got on her nerves. Never mind. Anna would just have to put up with her for one afternoon.

CHAPTER TWO

Josie was sitting up in her room later that day when she heard someone calling her name. Throwing open the window, she saw Anna standing on the path below, glossy dark hair falling back from her face as she squinted up into the sun.

"Locked in the tower, Rapunzel?" she called, laughing, as Josie held back her wavy auburn hair with one hand while she looked down.

"Ha-ha, very funny," Josie replied, feeling her spirits lift at once. She *had* been feeling rather lonely, all on her own in the empty house. "Hold on a minute. I'll come and let you in."

"It's so quiet in the yard now!" Anna exclaimed, following Josie down the hall. "Do you know it's been exactly a week since the party? Think how many people were here then."

Josie's dad had just staged the musical *Grease* at his school. When the performances were over, the Graces had thrown a big party at the stables. It was partly to thank everyone who'd been involved and partly to say good-bye to the students and friends who'd supported the stables over the years. Since that night, it seemed as though the place was really winding down. Charity's mother, Hope, had gone off the next day to begin her new life at Friendship House, a health center for physically challenged children. The horses who had lived at the school stables left the same weekend, too.

"It was a great evening, wasn't it?" Josie said, remembering all the fun. "I couldn't believe how many people showed up!"

"I know, it was great," Anna replied, as they climbed the stairs. "So, what's going on today?"

"Mom and Dad are off looking at houses and I'm under strict instructions to sort out my old stuff," Josie replied. "I can't go out for a ride until it's all done. Do you want to help?"

"Yes, definitely," Anna said excitedly. "Do you

think there's anything that would fit me?"

"I'm not sure," Josie said as they thudded up the stairs. "You're not that much smaller than me. Kirsty's probably the right size for most of the clothes. She's coming over later."

"Oh, Josie!" Anna said, making a face. "Why did you invite her? I thought it was just going to be the two of us. Kirsty always seems to be here these days, and she really gives me the creeps."

"I felt sorry for her," Josie confessed as they went into her bedroom. "I don't think she's got many friends. It's not the same for you, Anna—you're popular at school and you've got Ben to keep you company at home. I used to get lonely sometimes before you moved into the village, so I know how it feels."

"Feeling sorry for someone isn't a good way to start off being friends with them," Anna said, kneeling on the floor and sifting through a pile of Josie's old clothes. "Besides, the nicer you are to her, the more time she'll spend up here and soon you'll never be able get rid of her."

"Well, think of all the time you've spent here, Anna!" Josie exclaimed, sitting on the floor with her back against the bed. "You and Ben ended up helping out at the stables every weekend. Why shouldn't Kirsty?"

"But you like me, and you can put up with Ben," Anna said, holding a T-shirt up to the light and eyeing it critically. "I didn't think you felt the same about Kirsty. Anyway, she's younger than us, isn't she?"

"I think she's ten," Josie replied. "Oh, come on, Anna, let's change the subject. It won't kill you to be nice to Kirsty for an hour or so."

"You don't know that," Anna said darkly. "It might."

By the time Kirsty showed up, Josie had sorted out a pile of things she thought might fit her and Anna was lying on the bed, reading a magazine. She managed to give Kirsty a cheerful enough smile, though, and said hello nicely.

"Thanks, Josie," Kirsty said shyly, picking up a pair of jodhpurs and holding them against her skinny legs to see if they were long enough. "These look perfect!"

"I've got some jeans that might fit you, too,"

Josie said, dropping to her knees on the floor and picking them out of the heap. She could tell Kirsty felt awkward about taking too much. Soon, though, they'd filled a paper bag with clothes and a pair of riding boots Josie had grown out of.

"Are you sure you don't mind me taking all this?" Kirsty asked. "It'll be great to have some good clothes for riding." She got up and went over to the window. "I've never been in your room before," she went on. "It's got a great view! You can watch Charity outside and everything."

"Creep!" Anna mouthed in mock horror, looking at the piles of clothes all over the floor.

Josie threw her a death stare before replying, "It's kind of a mess at the moment, but I love it up here."

Kirsty started to rummage through a bag full of books under the window. "Oh, you're not throwing out your old horse stories, are you?" she said. "Don't you want to keep them?"

"Not really," Josie said, sprawling out on a beanbag. "I've read them so many times, I know them all by heart. Besides, I don't think I'm going to feel like reading about other people riding if I can't do it myself."

"But you can still do it yourself!" Anna said, putting down the magazine and swinging over her legs to sit up on the bed. "Even if you don't have Charity, we can go ride Faith. Jill invited us to visit her at the party, remember. And we can visit Hope at Friendship House, too. Mom's going to start working there next month, and she'll take us over there with her." Anna and Ben's mother, Lynne, was an artist, and since meeting Liz Tallant, who ran the respite center, she'd gotten the job as art teacher.

"I suppose so," Josie said doubtfully. "It's just that—"

She was interrupted by Kirsty, holding up a large hardcover book and asking curiously, "What's this?"

"Oh, it's a scrapbook I made a couple of years ago about Charity," Josie replied. "I found it last night when I was clearing out the bookcase. You can take a look, if you want."

The book was filled with dozens of photos of Charity, charting the first five years of her life. There were captions under each picture and lots of information about the horse's health and the food she ate, the prizes she'd won at the horse shows, and all her likes and dislikes.

"Wasn't she a cute foal?" Kirsty said, admiring the photos on the first few pages. "And there she is, suckling from Hope. That is so sweet!"

Josie smiled and then frowned sternly at Anna, who was silently putting her fingers down her throat, pretending to be sick. She looked over Kirsty's shoulder at the album. "I remember that day," Josie said, pointing to a picture of Charity wearing a saddle and a very suspicious expression. "She hated the saddle to begin with! And, look, there I am, sitting up on her. I was the first person to ride her, you know, when she was four."

"You look so young there!" Anna said, becoming interested in spite of herself and craning her head over to see the photo, too. "It must be the bangs and those chubby little cheeks."

"Well, it was four years ago," Josie said, giving her a playful shove. "I was only eight. What do you expect?"

Soon they had leafed through the entire book, and Kirsty closed it gently. "I just can't believe Charity's going to be sold," she said, looking seriously at Josie. "Won't your parents find the money for you to keep her somehow?"

"They might not able to," Josie said, inwardly wishing Kirsty would stop talking about it. She was just making her feel worse. "Look, we can't possibly afford to keep Charity at a boarding stable, and we don't have the money to move to a house with a field. So the simple fact is that Charity has to go."

"No!" Kirsty said. "I won't let them take her away from you!"

Something about her pale, determined face made Josie feel slightly uneasy. "Listen, Charity's going to be advertised in the paper on Wednesday," she told Kirsty firmly, "and we don't have any choice but to wait and see what happens after that."

"Bye, then," Josie said to Anna and Ben as they all got off the bus after school on Wednesday afternoon. She waved and started to turn away from the village and up toward Grace's Stables.

"Hang on!" said Anna, hurrying after her. "We're coming with you."

"We thought you might need some moral support," Ben added, getting a soccer ball out of his bag and kicking it ahead as he walked along. "Charity's being advertised today, isn't she?"

"That's right," Josie said, touched that they'd remembered. "You might get a bit bored, though," she went on. "There's not much to do at home these days. Now that there's only Charity left, Mom and I are arguing over who's going to muck her stall out."

"Well, we can just hang out and watch some TV or something," Anna said. "At least you won't be moping around on your own."

"Thanks," Josie said, giving her a grateful smile. "Everything does feel strange at the moment, like we're in a sort of limbo. I'm just trying not to think about what's going to happen. I've already decided I'm not going to look at the paper."

They walked into the yard. Charity, who was standing in her stall, neighed, just as she always did when Josie came back from school. "She looks so lonely, all on her own," Anna said as they made a big fuss about her. "She must be missing Hope and Faith."

"I'm sure she is," Josie agreed. "I was watching her in the field last night, and she doesn't seem to know what to do with herself." She sighed. "I should be hoping we get a new home quickly, for her sake, but in reality, I want to keep her for as long as possible. She's always been my special horse, from the moment she was born. It was hard enough saying good-bye to Faith and Hope, but I don't know how I'm going to manage it with Charity. It's not fair—this is her home, here with us!"

"But you're not going to be here for much longer, are you?" Ben asked as they went into the cottage. "Don't you have to move out of School Farm soon?"

"Yes, and we still don't know where we're going," Josie told him grimly. "Dad's got some real-estate agent friend who told him there were loads of property to rent on the market, which is why they left it until this late, but he and Mom have been looking for almost two weeks and nothing's turned up. I think Mom's getting worried."

"Mom's getting worried about what, exactly?" Mrs. Grace asked, looking up from the paper as the three of them came into the kitchen. She gave Ben and Anna a smile. "Hi there, you two!"

"Worried about where we're going to live," Josie told her after the twins had said hello. "You must be. We've got to be out of here in only two weeks."

"Yes, I am," Mrs. Grace admitted. "From what Jim had told Dad, I thought we'd have no trouble finding a house, but there's hardly anything around that we can afford! I don't think he realized what a tight budget we're on. Still, he's promised to let us know the second anything suitable turns up."

Josie got some apple juice from the fridge and put it on the table with three glasses and the cookie jar, trying to avoid looking at the newspaper. Her mother must have realized how she felt, because she hastily gathered the paper together and folded it up. "No houses in there today, anyway, and no jobs for me, either," she said, and then went on casually, "Charity's ad has gone in, but we haven't had any phone calls yet."

Josie nodded, sitting down at the table with Ben and Anna, who began to pour drinks for them all. She idly picked up some papers from the real-estate agent that had been hidden underneath the newspaper. "What are these, Mom?" she asked, looking at the photos of identical-looking houses on each one and reading the information typed below.

"Some places I had looked at today," Mrs. Grace replied. "None of them were ideal, but I think this one is the best of the bunch so far." She took a sheet from the pile Josie was holding and put it on the top.

"This one's the best?" Josie said, reading through the details and feeling her spirits sink even lower. "What makes you say that?"

"Because it's in between Dad's school and yours, it's inexpensive, and it's got three good-sized bedrooms," her mother replied. "All these modern houses are packed together very tightly, but there's actually a lot of room inside."

Josie turned over the sheet and then looked up at her mother, horrified. "Mom!" she exclaimed. "It says there's a 'small backyard.' What about all our animals? How can we fit Basil and the cats, plus all the ducks and chickens, in a small backyard?"

"We can't," her mother replied in a final tone. "I'm sorry, Josie. We're just going to have to accept that things won't be exactly the same as they are now. Of course, Basil and the cats can come with us—luckily he's not a big dog, and I'll walk him every day—but there's no way we can keep the ducks and chickens. It's simply not an option."

"Oh, great!" Josie said angrily. "That's wonderful news." She knew she wasn't behaving very well, but she couldn't help herself. It all seemed so unfair.

"*We've* only got a small backyard," Ben said

mildly, eating a cookie. "But it's better than nothing."

"The thing is, sweetheart," her mother went on, "we've gotten out of touch with reality, living here for years on such a low rent. We've been lucky to have a house like this for so long. Now it's time to join the real world."

"I should have seen this coming, I guess," Josie said gloomily, reading through the house details again.

"Come on!" Anna said. "It might not be too bad. Our mom will help decorate the place, and you know how good she is at making houses look wonderful."

"She can't do much with a small backyard, though, can she?" Josie grumbled.

"Look, Kirsty's coming for her lesson in half an hour," Mrs. Grace said brightly. "Why don't you saddle Charity and get her warmed up in the schooling ring? That might take your mind off things."

"I thought she only had lessons on the weekends," Josie said.

"I said I'd throw in a couple of extra ones for free

before we really do have to close," Mrs. Grace replied. "She's so fond of Charity. It's a pity the Fishers can't buy her. I'm sure they could afford to keep her boarded somewhere."

"So why won't they?" Josie asked, draining the last of her apple juice.

"I don't think anyone in that family is really interested in Kirsty's riding," said her mother. "She's so eager and she's been coming here every weekend for ages, but she still doesn't have her own riding hat. And seeing as the Fishers live in a big house with two expensive cars, it can't be the money."

At that moment, the phone began to ring outside in the hall.

"Let's go!" Josie said to Ben and Anna, jumping to her feet. She didn't feel like hearing her mother talk to all those lucky people who were looking for a horse to buy. One of them would probably end up taking her beloved Charity away, and that was something she just didn't want to think about.

CHAPTER THREE

"Bye, Mom!" Josie called as she swung lightly up into Charity's saddle. "See you later."

"Hang on a minute," Mrs. Grace said, putting aside the broom she'd been using to sweep the yard and hurrying over. "You haven't said where you're going yet."

"Oh, no—I forgot. Sorry!" Josie replied, sorting out the reins.

"You know how important it is for me to know where you'll be," her mother said. "How many times do I have to remind you?" It was one of Mary Grace's strict rules. She insisted on knowing the route anyone going out riding planned to take, in case of an accident.

"Sorry!" Josie said again, shifting her leg forward and reaching under the saddle flap to check Charity's girth. "I thought we'd cut through the fields and then along the river as far as the boathouse and back. It shouldn't take more than a couple of hours."

"I hope it doesn't," her mother said, giving the horse a pat and a quick inspection. "There are some more people coming to see Charity this afternoon, remember? The Taylors. I want her looking nice and fresh when they arrive."

"Okay," Josie called over her shoulder as she rode off down the path. It was a sunny Saturday morning and, despite all her worries, she couldn't help feeling a surge of happiness. "I'm going to forget everything for a couple of hours and just enjoy myself," she told Charity, and the horse's ears flicked back and forth alertly as if she agreed that was exactly the right thing to do.

The mare trotted smartly along the road, her tail swishing jauntily behind her. Josie soon found her rhythm, enjoying the fresh air and sunshine while she kept a steadying hand on the reins. When they turned off the road into a field that sloped gently uphill, she let Charity take off in a gallop. There was nothing to beat that wonderful feeling of flying over the ground, with the wind in your face and the sun on your back.

Before long they had reached the woods at the top of the hill. Now that Charity had worked off some of her energy, she was happy to trot steadily through the woods, and then down a lane and along a path that led to the river. Apart from one solitary fisherman sitting on the bank and staring out at the water, there was no one in sight. Not many people came to this stretch of the river because it was far from the road and took a while to reach on foot. It was quiet and peaceful, and one of Josie's favorite places. She used to come here often with the twins. Anna always rode Hope, and Ben would follow behind on steady old Faith—when he wasn't riding Tubber, his favorite among horses who were boarded at the stables.

Josie smiled to herself as she remembered some of the fun they'd had. A couple of miles farther on was the abandoned boathouse that they'd discovered on one of their first rides out together. They'd enjoyed exploring its interior until Ben put his foot through one of the floorboards, and Mrs. Grace declared the place out of bounds.

On one side of the boathouse stood two rooms that were in fairly good condition, with a couple of benches and even a decaying life jacket under one of them. An unsteady-looking veranda wrapped around the back room, raised on stilts over the river racing along beneath. The other half of the building, a large room where the boats would have been kept, hadn't lasted so well. A corner of the outside wall had rotted away altogether and most of the roof was gone, making a kind of open, grassy courtyard.

Josie rode on until she reached the boathouse, which lay in between the path and the river. She brought Charity to a halt, and they stood for a while, watching the water as it swirled in the grip of a powerful current. "I wish we could stay here forever, just you and me," Josie whispered, stroking the horse's silky smooth neck. Aware that this might be one of the last times they'd ride out here together, she gave a deep sigh, and then turned Charity around to take her back to the stables.

Mrs. Grace was working in the office and came out

to greet them when Josie trotted into the yard. "Good ride?" she said, giving Charity a pat.

"Great, thanks, Mom," Josie replied, dismounting. "Do you mind just holding Charity for a second while I take off her tack?"

"No problem," her mother replied, looping the reins over Charity's neck. "Could you let her out when you've finished, though, instead of putting her in the stall? The Taylors want to see how easy she is to catch, so they've asked to watch us bringing her in."

"Oh, okay," Josie said, running up the stirrup leathers before she took Charity's saddle off. "That's fair enough, I guess." If she was buying a horse, that was exactly what she'd want to do. "What are the Taylors like?" she asked when she'd come back from the tack room with a head collar. "Do they know anything about horses?"

"They certainly seem to," her mother said. "They've got an older boy who's had a horse for a while, and now they want a horse for his younger sister. She's been having riding lessons for ages."

Josie unbuckled Charity's bridle and quickly slipped on the head collar. "Thanks, Mom," she said, tying the rope to a ring on the wall. "I'll just sponge her down and give her a rub-over before she goes back out in the field. She might not be looking so clean by the time they arrive, though."

"Oh well, I don't think that should bother them too much," said Mrs. Grace, taking the bridle from her and going to hang it up in the tack room. "Lunch in an hour or so—Dad's making lasagna."

"Okay," Josie replied. Her father was a great cook and lasagna was one of his specialties, but she was beginning to feel nervous and the appetite that she had worked up while riding suddenly disappeared. The Taylors were the first people to come to see Charity. It sounded like they were serious about buying her, and the moment when she'd finally have to leave was drawing closer and closer.

The Graces were tidying up after a quiet lunch, when they heard a car pull up in the yard. "I think that must be the Taylors," said Mrs. Grace, putting down her napkin and taking Josie's arm to shepherd her out of the kitchen. "Come on, let's go and say hello."

Josie took a long, careful look at Emily Taylor as she got out the car, a girl about her own age with short brown hair. They might be selling Charity, but she wasn't prepared to let her horse go to anybody she didn't trust. Emily smiled hello rather shyly, but Josie decided that was okay. There would have been nothing worse than a know-it-all. Matthew, Emily's older brother, looked uninterested, but, since he wouldn't be the one looking after Charity, Josie felt it didn't matter so much what he was like.

"Well, should we go out to the field?" Mrs. Grace said, after they'd all said hello. "I'm sure you want to see Charity."

Josie found herself walking next to Emily on the way over to the field while her mother chatted with Mr. and Mrs. Taylor and Matthew wandered along on his own. "You're so lucky to live at a riding stable," Emily said, breaking the slightly awkward silence. "That would be my dream come true!"

"I've been lucky, I guess," Josie said. "But we've got to move soon because the stables are being sold. That's why we have to find a new home for Charity."

"Oh, I'm sorry," Emily said, blushing pink. "I didn't realize. How stupid of me!"

"It's all right," Josie said. "You couldn't have known. Don't worry about it." And she gave Emily a smile to show there were no hard feelings. "There she is," she added, waving a hand toward Charity, who was grazing in a corner of the field.

Emily caught her breath as she stared eagerly over. "Oh, she's beautiful!" she exclaimed. "I've been trying to imagine what she'd look like ever since we saw your ad in the paper. She's even better than I dreamed she'd be! Don't you think so, Matthew?"

"I guess so," her brother replied. "But you can't tell much from appearances. Wait till you've ridden her."

Josie started to speak and then stopped and bit her lip. She was so proud of Charity that she couldn't help wanting to tell them both what an utterly wonderful and marvelous horse she was. On the other hand, she still had a last wild hope that if the Graces couldn't sell Charity, she'd somehow be able to stay with them. She decided not to say anything that would encourage the Taylors to buy her.

"What do you think, Emily?" said Mrs. Taylor. "She looks all right, doesn't she?"

"She's beautiful!" Emily repeated. Josie took one

look at her face and realized nothing she said or didn't say would make the slightest difference—Emily had already fallen for Charity.

"Come on," Josie said, starting to open the gate into the field. "Let's catch her, and then you can see what she's like to ride."

As if she knew her every move was being watched, Charity behaved perfectly. She neighed and trotted up to the two girls as they walked over, allowing Emily to pat her while Josie slipped on her head collar. "Here you are," Josie said, handing Emily the lead rope. "Do you want to take her back to the yard and we can get her saddled up?"

"Yes, please," Emily said enthusiastically, giving Charity one last stroke and then leading her confidently back across the field, a broad smile on her face.

"Now don't make your mind up right away, Emily," Mrs. Taylor warned her when they reached the gate. "Matthew's right. You need to see how you feel about riding Charity. Take your time. This is a big decision."

Mary Grace gave Josie's hand a quick squeeze as

they all leaned on the fence around the outdoor schooling ring, watching while Emily put Charity through her paces. Josie was used to seeing other people on Charity, but this was desperately hard to take. "She's my horse, really!" she wanted to shout. "*I* should be riding her, not you!" Somehow, she managed to stifle the urge.

"She obviously knows how to ride," Mrs. Grace murmured in her ear, and Josie had to agree. Emily had gotten Charity moving in a good, balanced trot and, without any fuss, was making sure the horse did exactly as she was told. Charity was wonderful to ride but she was also "forward going," as Mrs. Grace put it—she didn't need much encouragement to go faster. It was obvious she wanted to canter now, but Emily firmly reined her back. Then at the next corner, when she was ready, she gave Charity the gentlest of touches with her heels and they struck off into a graceful canter.

"Looks like they're made for each other," Josie heard Mrs. Taylor say to her husband. Even Matthew commented, "That's not a bad little horse. Em could do a lot worse."

Enough was enough. Muttering something vague

to her mother, Josie turned on her heel and walked back to the cottage. She didn't want to make a fool of herself in front of the Taylors, but she just couldn't bear to watch Emily and Charity together any longer. It was like some awful sort of torture.

"Oh, Josie!" her father said as she stomped down the hall after flinging open the front door with a crash. "I'm so sorry. They're getting along well, aren't they?"

Josie nodded, pushing his arm away while she struggled to hold back the tears and control herself. "This is *so* hard!" she eventually managed to say as she paced up and down the kitchen.

"I know," her father said sympathetically. "And I wish I could do something to help! Listen, why don't we ask the Taylors whether you could ride Charity every now and then?"

"No," Josie said, sitting down at the table and burying her head in her arms. "I think that would only make things worse," she went on in a muffled voice. "I'll get over this, Dad, but not just yet. Right now, this is the worst thing that's ever happened in my life!"

CHAPTER FOUR

Josie heard a gentle tap on her bedroom door an hour or so later and then her mother's voice asking, "Are you okay?"

"Yes," she called, giving her mom a wan smile as she came into the room. "I'm sorry," she said, sitting up. "I know it must have looked bad, me rushing off like that, but seeing Emily on Charity suddenly really got to me."

"It's okay," said Mrs. Grace, perching on the bed next to Josie and stroking her thick, coppery hair. "Everyone understands how you feel. Emily said she'd be exactly the same if she had to part with her horse."

"She was all right, wasn't she?" Josie said. "I

didn't really want to like her, but I couldn't help it."

"Yes, she was," Mrs. Grace sighed. "And her parents were fine, too. I was half-hoping there'd be some reason why we couldn't let them buy Charity, but I couldn't find a single one. There are stables and a field not far from their house, with a couple of other horses there to keep her company. Emily's a good rider, too, and you can tell she adores Charity already. It's just hard to accept that we finally have to let her go."

"Do the Taylors definitely want to buy her?" Josie asked.

"They'd like to," Mrs. Grace replied. "I told them a couple of other people were interested but hadn't come to a decision, and they asked us not to sell her without calling them first. Before they say yes for certain, though, they've asked if they can have her seen by a vet, just to make absolutely sure she's okay."

"And we know she will be," Josie said gloomily, "so that's that."

"Looks like it," her mother replied. "I think the Taylors are really interested. They offered to leave part of the money for Charity in advance, but I've given my word we won't sell her to anyone else before she's passed her health check. They've got a friend who's a vet, and they'd like her to come by as soon as she can next week."

"Well, I guess if we've got to sell Charity to anyone, it might as well be them," Josie said, getting up from the bed and walking over to the window.

"I think so," agreed Mrs. Grace. "We probably won't get a better offer. And they don't live very far away, so I'm sure you could go and visit her after we've moved to wherever we end up living. Emily did say you'd be welcome to ride her sometimes, if you wanted to."

"I don't know about that," Josie said, looking at Charity all by herself out in the field again. "It might make things worse, seeing her settled into a new home and having to leave her there. I'd rather remember her like she is now, here with us."

Her mother came over to the window, and they watched Charity together for a while. She was standing with her head up in the air, as though she were listening to some sound being carried on the wind.

"You can tell she's missing the other horses,"

said Mrs. Grace with a sad smile. She put her arm around Josie. "I know how much we're asking of you, having to give her up," she said. "And I can't stand the thought of saying good-bye to her myself."

"Oh, why did everything have to change?" Josie said, leaning her head on her mother's shoulder. "We were so happy before, with Faith, Hope, and Charity all together. Why couldn't things just stay the way they were?"

"Because life's not like that, I'm afraid," Mrs. Grace replied. "Come on, though. We've still got each other! And there are a lot of people much worse off than we are."

"I guess so," Josie said, nodding.

"Look, why don't you give Anna a call and see if she can come and sleep over?" her mother suggested. "We could rent a video to watch, if you like."

"That's a good idea," Josie said, brightening a little. "Let's go for a comedy, though. I don't think I could face anything too serious tonight."

"Well, here's something to cheer us all up!" said Robert Grace, coming into the kitchen. "That was Jim on the phone."

Anna's mother, Lynne, had just dropped her off to stay the night, and they were all sitting in the kitchen eating cookies and milk. Lynne Marshall was one of Mary Grace's best friends, and they had as much to talk about as Josie and Anna.

"Oh, yes?" Mrs. Grace said, pulling out a chair and pouring a glass for her husband. "We could use some good news."

"Who's Jim?" asked Lynne Marshall.

"He's a real-estate agent friend of mine," Mr. Grace explained, taking a sip. "He promised he'd let us know if he heard of any good properties to rent, and it sounds like one might just have appeared."

Josie listened intently. She'd been denying the fact that in a couple of weeks they'd have to move, but it looked like now it was time to face up to it.

"Tell us more," Lynne was saying. "What's the place like?"

"Jim hasn't even seen it yet," Mr. Grace said, "so he couldn't go into much detail. The owner only came in this morning."

"Well, he must know something!" Mrs. Grace exclaimed. "Come on, Rob. Don't keep us in suspense!"

"Is it like those other houses you've been looking at?" Anna asked, exchanging a meaningful look with Josie.

"No, it isn't," said Mr. Grace. "That's the interesting part. It's pretty different, in every way." He sat back smugly, obviously having decided to enjoy teasing them for a while, much to Josie's irritation.

"Dad, I can't stand this anymore!" she burst out, jumping up and attacking him from behind. "If you don't tell me everything you know right now, I'm going to tickle you to death!"

"Okay, okay! I give in," her father gasped, laughing as he tried to defend himself. When Josie had gone back to her seat, he went on, "Well, the house is old, for a start. It used to be the gatehouse for some stately home that was knocked down years ago."

"And are you prepared to tell us where it is, exactly?" Mrs. Grace asked.

"On the other side of Littlehaven, just off the main road. It would be easy for Josie to get the bus into school," Mr. Grace replied. "The bad news is, it's not as big as some of the houses we've seen.

There are three bedrooms, but one of them is tiny, and the kitchen's not enormous, either."

"That doesn't bother me much," Mrs. Grace smiled. "You know how I feel about cooking."

"Our kitchen's minuscule," Lynne added. "You just have to train yourself to be neat."

"What's the good news, then?" Josie asked. "If the house is so small, why are you getting worked up about it?"

"Quick thinking, clever daughter of mine," said her father, taking the last cookie. "Well, apparently the house has a big yard and it's in a beautiful setting. I think that makes up for a small kitchen, don't you?"

"Mmm," Josie said thoughtfully. "That does sound nice."

"It sounds terrific!" said Anna, beaming at her. "When are you going to see it? Can we come, too?"

"It's empty at the moment because they've been having some work done, and Jim's got the keys so he can show people around," Mr. Grace said. "He's completely booked up with appointments at the moment, but he did say that we could take a quick look on our own if we wanted—seeing as he knows us. The realty office is closed tomorrow, but maybe we could go on Monday after school."

"Why don't we go now?" Anna suggested. "Someone else may have snapped it up by then!" She looked at her watch. "Come on, there's at least an hour until the office closes for the weekend, isn't there? We can pick up the keys and go straight there."

"Yes, why don't we, Dad?" Josie said. Now that she had started thinking about moving and was getting involved, she was curious to see the house. "Besides, if we go now, Lynne can come, too, and tell us how to make it look nice. You will, won't you?" she asked, looking appealingly at Anna's mother.

"I'd love to," Lynne replied, draining her cup of tea. "Ben's playing soccer, so I've got a few hours to spare, and you know how much I like poking around other people's houses."

"What do you think, Mary?" Mr. Grace asked his wife. "Do you want to go now?"

"Absolutely!" she replied, unhooking her shoulder bag from the doorknob. "Time's running out and we can't afford to miss a chance like this. Anyway, on Monday I've arranged for all of us to look at that other house I found. It would be useful to have seen this one first, because we need to make a decision in the next few days."

"Then let's not waste any more time!" Josie said, jumping up.

"This must be it," said Mr. Grace, pulling off the main road through a pair of tall iron gates and parking outside a cottage covered in terra-cotta tiles. He squinted at the sign next to the front door. "Yes, Lime Tree Lodge. Can anybody see a lime tree?"

Josie got out of the car and stared at the house. There was no yard in the front, and the main door opened straight on to the pavement. To the left, a black-painted wooden bench had been built into the wall, and on the other side of the door was a big bay window with diamond-leaded panes of glass.

"I suppose that's where the gatekeeper would have waited for the carriages to come down the drive," said her father, nodding at the bench.

"I like it," said Josie, sitting down and making herself comfortable. She could imagine herself bringing a book out there in the summer, or chatting with Anna while they watched the world go by.

"What's up there, Dad?" she went on, pointing up the narrow road that stretched off into the distance with fields on either side of it.

"I think it's a modern estate," he replied. "Look, you can just see a couple of houses on the edge. It's not too built up around here, though—most of the land is still farmed."

"What are we waiting for? Let's go inside," said Mrs. Grace from the doorstep. "You can't tell much from out here."

It was strange, walking into an empty house that until recently had been somebody else's home. Even Anna spoke in a whisper as they walked around the ground floor. "It feels like someone's going to spring out and ask us what we're doing here," she hissed, and Josie nodded in agreement.

Lynne and Mary Grace had made a beeline for the kitchen. "Well, it's bigger than ours," Lynne said, looking around. "You couldn't get a table in here, but there's a dining room to eat in. I wonder if the owner would let you put an opening in the wall? Or an arched window between them would look good, with glass shelves."

"Now, hold on a minute," laughed Mrs. Grace.

"Don't get carried away! A coat of paint's the most I was thinking of."

"Let's go and explore upstairs," Anna said, taking Josie's arm. "You want to get the best bedroom, don't you?"

They made their way up to the first floor. "Well, this is big enough," Anna said, going into a bedroom overlooking the front of the house. Seconds later, she called out, "Oh, Josie, this is perfect! You've even got a walk-in closet for all your clothes!"

"All what clothes?" Josie asked, looking over Anna's shoulder. "My things wouldn't even fill up one corner, especially now I've cleared out all my old stuff. No, something tells me this is the room Mom and Dad would choose."

She went back out on to the landing and examined two other doors leading off it. One led to the bathroom, and the other to a tiny room not much bigger than the walk-in closet she'd just seen.

"You could just about fit a bed and a desk in here, I suppose," Anna said, poking her head in from the door. "You'd have to keep your clothes somewhere else, though, even if you don't have that many."

"But I'm sure there were meant to be three

bedrooms," Josie said, squeezing past Anna out on to the landing again. "Yes! There's another door here, in the corner. How could I have missed it?"

She opened the door, and together they looked up the steep, winding staircase behind it. "This must lead to the third bedroom," Anna said in a hushed voice. "Come on, let's go and see."

"Feels like we're intruding again," Josie whispered as they cautiously climbed the stairs and emerged in a large attic room with sloping ceilings. The faint sound of their parents moving around and chatting floated up from downstairs, but otherwise the room seemed cut off from the rest of the house. It was painted white, and sunlight streamed in through the two large loft windows overlooking the backyard.

"This is terrific!" Josie said, looking around with shining eyes. "Don't you think so, Anna? I can just imagine myself here."

"You haven't seen the best part yet," Anna replied, looking out the windows. "Come and see!"

Josie hurried over and gazed through the dusty glass at the cottage's long backyard below. There were a couple of sheds on the left, and flower beds waist-high in weeds curved around from the other side, with a tangle of shrubs and bushes beyond. The grass was very overgrown, but she could make out the borders of a lawn with a huge tree in the middle. Her father was sprawled underneath it, lying in the long grass with his hands behind his head and his eyes shut.

"Looks like Dad's found the lime tree!" she said to Anna, with a laugh. "Honestly, he's hopeless! He hasn't even been upstairs to look at the bedrooms."

"But have you seen what's on the other side of the yard?" Anna said eagerly. "There! Past those bushes at the end."

At the bottom of the yard was a fence and on the other side of that, a field. A field that seemed to stretch on for miles, with two horses grazing in it.

Josie felt her heart leap when she saw them. "Oh, Anna!" she said. "Are you thinking what I'm thinking? Do you think there might be room for a horse in that field?"

"Well, it would be worth talking to your mom and dad about it, at least!" Anna said. "I mean, it just seems so perfect, having a field right there. If Charity could share it with those horses, you wouldn't have to pay to board her somewhere else, after all!"

Josie's eyes lit up. Her parents couldn't deny her this chance, could they? "Come on!" she said to Anna. "Let's go and ask them right now!"

CHAPTER FIVE

"But it would be ideal, Mom!" Josie said despairingly. "There's a huge field right at the bottom of the yard. Wouldn't there be room for Charity there? We could easily find out who owns it and ask them if we could rent a space."

"I'm so sorry, sweetheart," her mother replied, looking anguished. "If there was any way of our keeping Charity, of course I'd say yes. But it isn't just a matter of living next to a field. It's what we'd have to pay for her feed, and shoeing, and vet's bills, and worming, and tack—and that's apart from the cost of renting the field. You know how expensive it is to keep a horse!"

"But what if we both got a job?" Anna asked,

looking from Josie to her mother. "There must be something we could do!"

"I don't think there is," Mary Grace replied. "It's not easy to find work around here, and I should know. I've been searching hard enough and I haven't come up with anything yet. You're not old enough to baby-sit yet, and something like a newspaper route wouldn't earn you enough."

"It can't just be a question of money!" Josie cried desperately.

"I'm afraid it is," said her father, his footsteps echoing on the bare floorboards as he walked into the room. "Things are going to be very difficult for us for a while, Josie. There'll be no income from the stables, and it may take some time before Mom can start working again. This house is at the top of our price range, and it's going to take every penny we've got. But even if we rented the cheapest one we've seen, we wouldn't have enough money left over to keep Charity."

"I'm so sorry," Mrs. Grace said again, putting a comforting arm around Josie's shoulder. "It must seem hard, but I think we'll have to put having a horse of your own on hold for a while. You never know, circumstances may change later on and things could be different."

But Charity will be sold by then, and she's the only horse I'll ever want! Josie felt like saying, desperately trying to make the lump in her throat disappear.

"We *could* find out who owns the field, though, and who the horses belong to," Mrs. Grace suggested. "Maybe they need someone to help look after them? And who knows, you might be able to do some riding, too."

"Never mind," Josie muttered. "I don't really want to." Not looking at anyone, she added, "I'm just going to sit on the bench for a while." She didn't want to be anywhere in sight of a field that would make a perfect home for Charity—not with her parents telling her there was no possibility of this great opportunity ever becoming a reality.

Everybody else had plenty to say in the car on the way home, so it was easy for Josie just to sit and stare out of the window. She didn't feel like joining in the conversation.

"I thought the cottage had a really comfortable,

friendly feeling about it," her mother was saying, turning around in the front passenger seat to talk to Lynne—"especially with that bench at the front! It seems so welcoming, somehow."

"I know what you mean," Lynne answered. "The paintwork needs touching up in places, but the house doesn't look at all uncared for and depressing, like some empty places do. The downstairs rooms might not be very big, but the two main bedrooms are good-sized."

"That loft room is great!" Anna said, flashing Josie a smile and squeezing her arm to try to cheer her up.

"It's the yard I like best," Mr. Grace put in. "I'm sure we could get it into shape over the summer vacation. Think of the picnics we could have under that tree! I'll get Jim to ask the landlord if we can keep the chickens in one of those sheds, and maybe he'll let us make a pond for the ducks."

"What do you think, Josie?" Mrs. Grace asked tentatively. "It's much better than those other houses, isn't it?"

Josie looked at her anxious face and suddenly felt a pang of guilt. Her mother was losing her job as well as her home, and having a depressed, grumpy daughter must only be adding to her worries.

"It's a lot better," she said, trying to summon up a smile.

"And you don't have to worry about a small backyard anymore," her mother added encouragingly. "We'll probably be able to keep all the birds, and Basil could play around in the bushes to his heart's content."

"Well, sounds like we're all agreed," Robert Grace said. "I'll call Jim at home when we get back and tell him we'll take it."

"And you'll have all of August to get settled in," Lynne said. "Your school year finishes on Wednesday, doesn't it?"

"Yes, it does," Josie said, halfheartedly. This must be the first summer vacation ever that she wasn't particularly looking forward to.

"I'm going to be working at Friendship House for a couple of days a week soon," Lynne said. "Why don't you and Anna come with me? You can help with the children and visit Hope. Oh, I forgot to tell you. I went in to talk to Liz Tallant yesterday and to say hello to Hope."

"Mom! You should have told us," Anna exclaimed. "How was Hope? Is she happy?"

"She looked wonderful," Lynne said cheerfully. "She's bossing around those two donkeys in her field like an old mother hen, and Liz says the children all love her to pieces."

"I bet they do," Josie said with a real smile this time, beginning to feel a little happier in spite of herself. "Dear old Hope. It would be great to see her again."

"Then let's do it!" Anna said. "That's a great idea, Mom. We could call Jill and arrange to go visit Faith over the summer, too."

"Yes, I think we should," Josie said, making a huge effort to be more positive. "And we can spend some time fixing up my room, and exploring—"

"And gardening," Mr. Grace added.

"And I won't be so busy, so we can all do things together," said Mrs. Grace. "I bet you'll find the summer flying by, Josie."

"Yes, maybe it will," Josie said, deciding then and there not to think too deeply about anything but just to get through the next few weeks as best she could.

* * *

The next day, Mary Grace brought out all the cardboard boxes she'd been collecting in the barn, ready to begin the task of packing up. "If we do some every day next week, we won't be completely exhausted by the time we have to leave," she said. "I'll start with your books on Monday, Rob."

Mr. Grace had spoken to the real-estate agent as soon as they'd gotten back from looking at the house. Now it was just a question of paying a deposit and signing the contract, and Lime Tree Lodge would be theirs to live in from the beginning of August, in ten days.

"Are you feeling better about things?" Anna asked Josie that morning while they were grooming Charity.

"I've decided to try and take each day as it comes," Josie replied, getting to work with the dandy brush on a patch of mud over Charity's withers. "I don't really want to think about the future too much."

"That's probably the best thing to do," Anna agreed. "Anyway, you've got nearly another week with Charity still, haven't you? That's good news." The Taylors had called earlier to say the vet they knew was away at a conference all week and wouldn't be able to check Charity over until Saturday morning.

"Besides," Anna went on, carefully brushing out Charity's mane, "you never can tell what the vet might find. I know!" she said suddenly, her face lighting up. "Why don't we bribe her to say Charity's got some awful disease?"

"That's a terrible idea," Josie said in dismay. "For a start, we've got nothing to bribe her with, and I bet she wouldn't agree if we had. And even if she did make something up—who'd believe her? The Taylors aren't stupid—they can see Charity's healthy and fit." It was true: Josie was spending so much time riding the horse and grooming her that she was in top condition.

"You're right. But it was worth a try," Anna admitted, not at all discouraged. "I'm surprised Kirsty is not here by now," she added, looking at the yard. "What time's her lesson?"

Josie checked her watch. "In about half an hour," she said. "When she does turn up, try not to say anything about us having found a buyer for Charity, okay? Mom thinks she'll be really upset and that we shouldn't tell her until it's definitely settled."

"You know me," Anna grinned. "I'm not one to blurt things out."

"Ha-ha," Josie said sarcastically. "That is a joke, isn't it? You've got the biggest mouth in the history of the world, Anna Marshall."

For the whole next week, Josie tried really hard to keep as calm as she'd told Anna she'd be. She floated through the last day of school on Wednesday and said good-bye to her friends, promising them she'd call with her new address and phone number. She continued riding Charity every day, feeding, grooming, and mucking out her stall. All the time she was telling herself not to think about what she'd be doing next week, when there wouldn't be a horse to look after anymore.

And then, before she knew it, Saturday had arrived and the Taylors' vet was parking her car in the yard. Mrs. Grace took her over to where Charity was waiting, tied up outside the stalls, while Josie hovered around in the background. She didn't want to miss anything, but at the same time, she wasn't in a hurry to hear Charity declared fit and well and able to be sold.

"Hello, there, gorgeous," the young woman said, giving the horse a stroke. "I can see why Emily was so taken with you. You're beautiful!"

She began to check Charity over, taking her temperature and her pulse and listening to her heart. Then she felt each of her legs for swelling or muscle damage, lifted up each hoof in turn to check her feet, and carefully opened her mouth to examine her teeth. Josie had to try to soothe Charity down at this point, because she'd begun to fidget and toss her head.

"That's all right," smiled the vet. "I don't like strangers poking around in my mouth, either. Could you take her for a quick trot on the lead rein now?" she asked Josie. "Just so I can watch how she moves."

At the end of the examination, she began to pack all her equipment away and gave Josie and her mother a smile. "That's one lovely horse," she said, "as I'm sure you already know. She's got tons of personality, hasn't she? There are no problems there that I can see, and I'm happy to let the Taylors know it. I'd just like to see her vaccination record, and then I'll pass her with flying colors."

"Of course," said Mrs. Grace. "It's down in the office with the rest of the paperwork. I'll show you the way. You could put Charity back in her stall, Josie," she added. "Kirsty is coming for a lesson this afternoon. It looks like we'll have to tell her it'll be the last one."

Josie led Charity back into the stable, feeling numb. So this was it. The final hurdle had been crossed and, unless a miracle happened, Charity would be going to the Taylors. It was like some horrible dream.

Mrs. Grace called the Taylors after lunch. "We've agreed that they'll come and pick Charity up on Tuesday," she said, coming into the stall where Josie was saddling up the horse for her lesson. "I thought you might like to keep her until just before we move."

"Okay," Josie said mechanically, buckling up the girth.

Mrs. Grace gave her a quick hug. Then she added, "I'll have a word with Kirsty after the lesson—I don't want to spoil it for her. And I think I might give her mother a call and ask her to take Kirsty home this time, rather than letting her walk back on her own. She might be pretty upset."

* * *

"That was wonderful!" Kirsty said to Josie, jumping down from Charity at the end of the lesson. "I didn't think your mom was going to let me start jumping yet!"

"Well, I did promise you could take Charity over a couple of jumps at some stage," said Mrs. Grace, walking up with Mrs. Fisher. "And it had to be this afternoon, Kirsty, I'm afraid. You know we have to leave the stables soon?"

Kirsty nodded, her eyes wide.

"Well, next week we're moving to our new house, and now we've found someone who wants to buy Charity. She'll be going to *her* new home next week, too."

"But I didn't realize," Kirsty stammered, looking desperately from Mrs. Grace to her mother to Josie. "I mean, I never thought you'd really . . ." Her eyes brimmed over with tears and she couldn't say anymore.

"Why don't you give the horse a hug good-bye?" Mrs. Fisher said. "This isn't the end of the world. You can continue having lessons at Littlehaven."

"It *is* the end of the world to me!" Kirsty blurted

out angrily to her mother. "What do you know about it? You don't understand anything!" And she turned and ran out of the yard.

"Kirsty!" her mother shouted after her. "Come back here!" Then she turned to Mrs. Grace. "I'm so sorry," she said, looking embarrassed. "I've been trying to tell her for weeks that this would happen, but she refused to believe me. I suppose she thought you couldn't ever bring yourselves to sell Charity."

Well, that makes two of us, Josie said grimly to herself. *I know exactly how you feel, Kirsty, if that's any consolation.*

"Poor Kirsty," Mrs. Grace said, when the Fishers had both gone. "Still, they've got some nice horses at Littlehaven. I'm sure she'll soon find one to take Charity's place."

"Maybe," Josie said shortly, starting to heave off the saddle. An unspoken thought hovered on the air between them: Charity couldn't ever be replaced, as far as the Graces were concerned.

"Look, why don't the two off us go out for a ride together tomorrow?" Mrs. Grace offered. "I could do with a break from packing, and I can ride Connie over from Littlehaven. Mary's asked me to take her out." Connie was the black mare who used to be boarded at Grace's Stables. Mrs. Grace had continued exercising her, even though she'd moved to another place nearby.

"Okay," Josie said, buckling up Charity's head collar. "Whatever you like." She couldn't bring herself to feel that anything mattered, not even how they spent these last few days. Charity was going, and nothing could alter that final, awful fact.

Josie spent a restless night. It was heavy, thundery weather, and her bedroom felt airless and stuffy. She tossed and turned, her mind racing with all kinds of strange dreams. At one point, she was with Charity at the airport, trying to load her on to the revolving luggage belt. Her hooves kept slipping on its smooth black surface. "This horse should be packed in a suitcase," the flight attendant was saying. "Why haven't you prepared her for the journey? The plane leaves in ten minutes."

She woke up early in the morning, feeling anxious and panicky. Finding her way between the half-filled boxes that covered her bedroom floor, she looked out of the window, hoping the sight of

Charity grazing quietly in the field would calm her down. The storm clouds had broken, and a misty gray drizzle hung in the air. But Charity was nowhere to be seen.

Josie rubbed her eyes, thinking she must be still half asleep, then looked again. There was no sign of the horse anywhere. She must be right over by that curve in the hedge, Josie thought, craning to see the outermost edge of the field. Quickly, she pulled on some jeans and a T-shirt and ran downstairs, grabbing a pair of boots from the porch on her way out of the house. Basil leaped out of his basket in the kitchen when he heard the door opening and scurried along beside her.

She climbed over the gate and ran toward the middle of the field. When she was certain she could see every inch of it, she stopped and looked around for some flash of white that would tell her Charity was there. Basil stopped to search, too, one paw lifted and his black nose sniffing eagerly. Josie's heart was thumping so loudly it threatened to burst out of her chest, and the palms of her hands prickled with sweat. Whirling around, she stared at every hollow, every corner, every bend in the hedge, before coming to the final conclusion she was almost afraid to make.

"Mom, Dad!" she screamed, running at top speed back toward the house. "Charity's gone! She's not in the field!"

CHAPTER SIX

"Maybe there's a gap in the fence somewhere that we haven't noticed," Mrs. Grace said, her dark curly hair already beaded with raindrops as she and Josie hurried toward the field. "Don't panic yet—she's probably not far away."

"But we checked the fence the other day!" Josie said frantically, searching for some sign of Charity. "I guess she could have found a weak spot in the hedge and got into the field where we used to board the horses. She's never done that before, though."

"I'll look in the jumping paddock and the yard," Mr. Grace called. The stripy pajama top he hadn't stopped to change billowed out over his jeans as he rushed toward the stalls.

Josie climbed over the damp, slippery fence around the field, too impatient to wait for her mother to open the gate. Her mind was racing with all sorts of horrible scenes—Charity lying in some ditch with a broken leg or a gash from a barbed-wire fence, or galloping on to a busy road, or maybe even being loaded into a trailer and taken off by some gang of thieves. Where on earth was she?

"Now, don't just rush off," Mrs. Grace said. "Let's get organized. I'll walk along the back hedge and see whether she might have got through at the side into the other field. Basil can come with me. He might pick up her scent. You look at the fence around the front and by the schooling ring. Don't worry, sweetheart, I'm sure we'll find her soon!"

"You don't think she might have been stolen, do you, Mom?" Josie asked, hardly daring to put her fear into words.

"Oh, I don't think so," her mother replied. "It's more likely she's wandered off somewhere."

Josie forced herself to slow down and look carefully along the boundary of the field for any broken posts or white hairs caught in the wood that would show where Charity might have broken through.

Maybe she realized we were going to sell her, she thought as she walked along, anxiously scanning the fence. Charity was so intelligent, she had probably picked up on the unusual atmosphere at the stables. First Faith and then Hope leaving must have worried her, too. Charity was lonely— they'd noticed how she seemed to be looking around for the other horses. Maybe now she'd gone to find them! Oh, why did we leave her on her own? Josie asked herself. Why didn't we guess something like this would happen?

She was jolted from her worries by a shout from her father, who was running over from the yard. "Come here!" he called urgently, waving to summon Mary Grace from the far end of the field as well.

"What is it, Dad?" Josie asked, scrambling back over the fence to join him. "Have you found something?"

"Yes and no," he replied breathlessly, his face pale. "I *haven't* found something would be more accurate." He took Josie's arm and hurried her over to the tack room. "There!" he said, pointing toward it.

"Oh, no!" Josie said, as she looked at the door swinging open. "I'm sure I locked up last night!"

"It's not that. Go inside," her father said, following closely behind her as she headed into the dark little room. Apart from a couple of spare head collars and a show saddle they didn't often use, it was empty. Charity's tack was gone.

Josie gasped and fell back against the wall. She felt as though someone had punched her in the stomach.

"You know what this means, don't you?" Robert Grace said, putting a steadying arm around her shoulders.

"Yes," Josie replied, in a voice that sounded to her own ears as though it were coming from very far away. "It means someone has *stolen* Charity."

At that moment, Mrs. Grace came through the door. She glanced around the bare tack room walls and then said grimly, "I think we'd better go back to the house, don't you? We'll need to call the police."

Josie and her father sat at the kitchen table while Mary Grace used the phone in the hallway.

"I can't believe it!" Josie said, sipping the hot sweet tea her father had made. "Why didn't we hear something? My bedroom overlooks the field, after all, and I didn't sleep very well last night."

"I just can't understand it," Mr. Grace said, holding his head in his hands. "I mean, why would the thief bother to take any tack? You'd have thought it wasn't worth the risk of getting caught."

Mrs. Grace came back into the kitchen and drew a chair up to the table. "Well, it's all official now," she said. "Charity's reported stolen, and we've even got a crime number." She looked in disbelief at the scrap of paper in her hand. "Impossible to take it all in, isn't it?"

"I'll pour you a cup of tea," Mr. Grace said, rubbing her back comfortingly. "That might make you feel better."

"What did the police say?" Josie asked. "Have any other horses in the area been reported missing?"

"Not so far," her mother replied. "At first they told me she'd probably just strayed, but her tack disappearing, too, made them take me seriously. It's odd, though. Apparently, horses are usually stolen just before an auction, and there aren't any around here, that I know of, for weeks."

"I hate thinking about someone creeping around

here and taking her off in the middle of the night," Josie said with a shudder. "Nothing like this has ever happened to us before."

"You don't think it could have something to do with our having advertised Charity in the paper, do you?" Mr. Grace asked his wife. "Could someone have come by and had a good look at the place, to check it out before coming back later?"

"But the Taylors were the only people who saw her," Mrs. Grace said, running her hands through her hair distractedly. "They didn't exactly look like horse thieves, did they? And we can easily trace them."

"We'll have to tell the Taylors what's happened if Charity doesn't turn up soon," Mr. Grace remarked. "Maybe we should call them if there's been no news by the end of the day."

"This is just horrible!" Josie said, pushing back her chair and pacing up and down the floor. "If anyone touches a hair on her head, I'll find out who they are and—well, I don't know what I'll do to them!"

"Don't worry, sweetheart," said her father, reaching around to squeeze her hand. "I'm sure whoever took her, won't hurt her. They're probably only in this for the money. And she's been freeze-branded with a number on her shoulder, hasn't she? We'll be able to identify her for certain if she turns up at a sale."

"Oh, yes! I completely forgot to tell the police about that," Mrs. Grace said. "I'm so worried, I can't think straight. Still, there's an officer coming by later to ask us questions and take a look at the field and the tack room. I'll mention it then."

"I'm going to call Anna and Ben," Josie said, going to the door. "I feel like talking to someone and there's nothing else we can do, is there?"

"Not that I can think of," said her mother. "We'll just have to sit here and wait for the police to arrive."

Josie dialed the Marshalls' number with shaking fingers. It was still early in the morning, and Anna sounded half asleep as she answered the phone. But when Josie told her what had happened, she immediately snapped to attention. "Stay right where you are!" she commanded, though Josie wasn't planning on going anywhere. "I'll wake Ben up and we'll be around before you know it."

Josie put down the receiver and went back

through to the kitchen. Her parents were just sitting there in silence. They seemed to be in a state of shock, and she knew exactly how they felt. "I'm going to have another look around till Ben and Anna get here," she told them. "Maybe I can pick up some clues."

"Well don't touch anything," her mother warned. "Just tell the police if you find anything—they're the experts."

"Okay," Josie said, heading out of the house. She stared at the empty field, trying to re-create what must have happened in her mind. Why would someone run the risk of coming right up to the riding stables? If they were going to steal a horse, why not pick one in an isolated field, miles from anywhere, where they could drive up with a trailer, load the horse in, and get away really quickly.

There was no need to look for weak spots in the fence now, but Josie walked along it anyway as far as the gate, keeping her eyes open for any little thing that shouldn't have been there—a patch of grass that had been flattened, perhaps, or a scrap of material or paper. She found nothing. Everything looked just as it usually did, except for the fact that Charity was gone. It was as though she'd been spirited away by magic.

She combed the yard next, her eyes fixed to the ground, and then looked in the stalls before turning her attention to the tack room. Jamming her hands in her pockets to remind herself not to touch anything, she looked at the open door. It had been unlocked, not forced open, and the key was still in the lock. The flowerpot under which it was always hidden was neatly back in its place.

Josie was staring at the tack-room door when Ben and Anna arrived on their bikes. Anna jumped off and flung hers against the office wall, her eyes wide with concern. "Josie! Are you okay?" she gasped breathlessly. "What's happening? Where are the police?"

"They're coming later," Josie told her.

"When did this happen?" Ben asked, following close behind his sister. "Did you hear anything? Was it a gang?"

"No, it must have happened in the middle of the night," Josie replied. "And I don't think it was a gang. Whoever stole Charity took her tack as well."

"You wouldn't have thought they'd bother, would you?" Ben said, frowning.

"And that's not the only thing," Josie said,

pointing to the tack-room door. "They unlocked the door with the key from under the flowerpot. How did they know where it was kept?"

"Maybe a lucky guess?" Anna suggested.

"But why waste time fumbling around in the dark, searching for a key, when it would be quicker to simply force the door open?" Josie replied. "No, I think whoever it was knew exactly where to find that key."

"So you think the person who's stolen Charity is someone who knows the stables well?" Anna said. "That's awful!"

"It is, isn't it?" said Josie slowly, thinking the whole thing over. An image of herself, bending down to take the key from its hiding place, had suddenly flashed into her head. The beginning of an idea was taking shape at the back of her mind but, as it seemed so far-fetched, she dismissed it at once.

"Here come the police," Ben said. "You can tell them all about it."

A black-and-white car drove up and parked in the yard. Two officers got out: a burly, middle-aged man and a younger woman, who had been driving.

Josie walked over to meet them, while Ben and

Anna hung back. "Hello, I'm Josie Grace. Thanks for coming so quickly," she said. "My parents are in the house."

"I'm Sergeant Bryant and this is Detective Hutchins," said the man, looking surprised. "But I think there's been some misunderstanding. Were you expecting us?"

"Yes," Josie answered. "My mother called the police station a little while ago. You've come about our horse, haven't you?"

"No, as a matter of fact, we haven't," said Sergeant Bryant, looking around the yard as he spoke. "What's happened to this horse of yours?"

"Well, she's been stolen," Josie stammered, looking at the two police officers in surprise. "Why are you here, if you haven't come about that?"

"It might be best if we all go indoors so we can talk to your parents," Sergeant Bryant said. "We can explain everything there."

"But what's happened?" Josie asked in alarm. "Has there been an accident or something?"

"Don't worry, Josie," the woman officer told her kindly. "It's nothing like that. We're making inquiries about a young girl who's been reported missing, that's all, and we think you and your parents might be able to help us."

Josie stared at her without speaking. That crazy idea in the back of her mind forced its way to the front. "A young girl?" she repeated faintly.

"That's right," said Sergeant Bryant. And when he spoke her name, Josie found that she wasn't the least bit surprised. "Kirsty Fisher," he said. "She was here yesterday afternoon, wasn't she?"

CHAPTER
SEVEN

"So you think that Kirsty Fisher's disappearing at the same time as your horse isn't just a coincidence?" Sergeant Bryant asked Josie. The two police officers were now sitting around the kitchen table with her parents and they were all drinking cups of tea as the Graces answered the officers' questions.

"The two things *have* to be connected!" Josie said, leaning forward over the table in her eagerness to convince the sergeant. "It all adds up! To start off with, we know Kirsty's crazy about Charity. When we told her that Charity was going to her new owners next week, she was really upset, so she must have decided to try and do something about it."

Sergeant Bryant looked across at Detective

Hutchins, who was busy taking notes, and raised his eyebrows. "And how do you think she took the horse?" he asked, turning back to Josie.

"Kirsty watched me unlock the tack-room door a couple of weeks ago, so she saw where we hide the key," Josie told him. "She obviously came back last night, took Charity from the field, saddled her up, and rode her away. That's why we didn't hear anything! Charity is used to Kirsty, and she would have gone quietly with her."

"But Kirsty hasn't ever caught Charity before," Mrs. Grace objected. "Do you really think she'd have tried to do it in the middle of the night like that? She's such a shy, quiet little thing."

"Creepy, more like," Anna snorted. Mrs. Grace gave her a sharp look, and Detective Hutchins glanced up from her notebook. "Sorry," Anna said, a little shamefaced. "But it's a really deceitful thing to do to your friends, isn't it?"

"I'm sure if Kirsty has taken Charity, she didn't do it to spite us," Mrs. Grace replied.

"Whatever she has or hasn't done," Sergeant Bryant added, "we have to concentrate on finding her as quickly as we can, before things get worse."

"Kirsty has caught Charity before, anyway," Josie said, picking up the thread of the conversation in the silence that followed his words. "She came with me into the field that day and I showed her how. Come on, Mom, remember how upset she was yesterday! She must have thought this was her last chance to save Charity."

"Yes, Mrs. Fisher said she was beside herself," Detective Hutchins put in, looking back over her notes. "That's why she knew something must have been wrong when she saw Kirsty's empty bed this morning."

"You don't think Kirsty could have just gone around to a friend's house without telling her parents?" Mr. Grace asked.

"Well, her mother's called everyone she can think of, but no one's seen her," Detective Hutchins replied. "She told us Kirsty doesn't have many friends, anyway. Oh, by the way, I think you need to check your phone. Mrs. Fisher says she tried to call you right away to see if Kirsty was here, but she couldn't get hold of you."

"That's strange. We used it this morning," Mr. Grace said, frowning as he went out to the hall.

Seconds later, he was back. "Mystery solved," he announced. "The receiver was off the hook—it hadn't been put back properly."

"Oh, that must have been me!" Josie said. "I was so nervous when I called you, Anna, I must have not paid attention."

"Now let me just make sure I've got this straight," Sergeant Bryant said heavily. "You told Kirsty yesterday afternoon that her favorite horse was going to a new home. She left here very upset at about four o'clock, and you haven't seen her since. No one heard or saw anything unusual in the night, but you found the horse gone about seven this morning and reported it to us half an hour or so afterward. A head collar and the saddle and bridle were also missing, and the tack-room door was unlocked. Is that it?"

The Graces nodded and he went on. "Well, let me know if you remember anything else that seems significant. I'll have to let the station know we might be looking for a girl on horseback—it'll make a difference to the area we search." He got up from the table. "We'll just take a look at the field and the tack room on our way out. I'll get one of our fingerprint specialists to come over as soon as possible. You haven't touched anything, have you? Good."

"They probably haven't gone far," Detective Hutchins said reassuringly to Josie, Ben, and Anna as she followed the sergeant out with Mr. and Mrs. Grace. "And I'm sure we'll find them quickly."

"I hope so," Josie said, resting her head in her arms on the kitchen table. She suddenly felt absolutely exhausted.

"Don't worry," she heard Ben say, and glanced up to see him looking at her sympathetically. "After all," he added, "at least we know Charity hasn't been taken by a real thief."

"Well, Kirsty seems real enough to me," Josie answered. "And now I'm worried about what's happened to her, too. Still, I know what you mean."

Mrs. Grace poked her head through the kitchen door. "I'm just going to call Kirsty's mother and talk all this over with her," she said. "Dad's gone upstairs to take a shower. Why don't you three have some breakfast?"

"Oh, Mom, I couldn't eat a thing," Josie said. She still had a strange, empty feeling in her stomach, but she wasn't the slightest bit hungry.

"Well, just help yourselves if you feel like it," her mother said, noticing that Ben was already reaching in the cupboard for a cereal box.

"I know we shouldn't be too hard on Kirsty when she could be lying injured somewhere," Anna said, after Mrs. Grace had gone out. "But if she has taken Charity, I still think it's a nasty thing to do. Especially when you've always been so kind to her, Josie."

"I've got a feeling she's trying to help me, in some weird way," Josie said. "When I first thought she might have taken Charity, I was really angry. And then I remembered some of the things she's said in the past, about helping me keep her. She thinks it's really unfair that Charity can't stay with us. Maybe she wanted to stop her from being sold, and didn't think about what would happen next."

"That's for sure," Ben said, pouring milk on to a big bowl of cornflakes. "Did she imagine your parents would just say, 'Oh, well, maybe we won't sell Charity after all, now that Kirsty's taken off with her'? And how long is she planning to stay on the run, do you think?"

"I don't know," Josie said, looking out of the

window at the rain that had begun to fall again. "I bet she's regretting it already. But where on earth is she?"

"Well, her mother's frantic," Mrs. Grace said, coming back into the kitchen. "She didn't want to talk to me for too long, in case the police were trying to get through with any news. But she did tell me that Kirsty's asthmatic, which I never knew. Apparently, she's taken her inhaler with her, but what if she has a really bad attack and there was no one around? I can't even imagine!"

"They've just got to find her!" Josie said anxiously, and even Anna began to look seriously worried.

"Why don't we go out on our bikes and help look?" she said. "We might be able to spot something."

"Then you really all should have something to eat," Mrs. Grace insisted. "I don't want to be sending out search parties for you, too."

The day passed very slowly. In the morning, Josie, Ben, and Anna went out on their bikes along the roads around the village. They were passed several times by police cars and saw officers on doorsteps making door-to-door inquiries. There was no trace of a blond-haired girl on a gray horse, though, and cycling along in the rain made them feel tired and depressed. They couldn't get far across the fields, either, which they all agreed was probably the way that Kirsty would have gone.

"After all, she wouldn't ride along the road, would she?" Ben said. "She must realize everyone will be out looking for her by now."

"We might as well go back home," Josie said. "I don't think we're doing much good out here. Let's see if there's been any news."

"Any phone calls, Mom?" she asked as they trooped back into School Farm, but Mrs. Grace just shook her head.

"Only a couple for Dad, I'm afraid," she said. "The fingerprint man came, but he couldn't get any clear prints from the door frame. Now, you'd better get changed out of those wet clothes, sweetheart. Lynne's coming over for lunch. I'll call and tell her to bring some dry things for Ben and Anna."

Robert Grace had cooked roast chicken for lunch, with vegetarian sausages for Lynne. Apart from Ben, though, no one felt like eating much.

"So why did John Phillips have to call you up on a Sunday?" Mrs. Grace said to her husband, as they all sat around picking at their food.

"My demon headmaster?" Mr. Grace replied. "Oh, just something that's come up at school. I'll have to go in for a meeting tomorrow morning, I'm afraid. But it shouldn't take too long."

Tomorrow morning, Josie thought to herself. I wonder what will have happened by then? She could tell her mother was thinking along the same lines.

"I just hope they're not out in the open, that's all," Mrs. Grace said as she stared out of the kitchen window at the steadily falling drizzle. "It can't be doing Kirsty's asthma much good to be out in this damp weather."

"You wouldn't believe it was still July today, would you?" Lynne Marshall said, making an effort to be cheerful. "Still, it's been lovely and sunny up until now." She began to clear the scarcely touched plates of food.

"Rob and I thought we might go out for another look in the fields this afternoon," Mrs. Grace said, looking around the table. "Are there any other volunteers? I'm sure the police wouldn't mind some help with the search."

"I'm going to try and contact Horsewatch over the Internet at home," Anna said. "It's a Web site especially for lost and stolen horses. Do you want to come, too, Josie?"

"No thanks," she replied. "I'd rather stay here by the phone, just in case there's any news, if that's okay with you." Suddenly, a new anxiety occurred to her. "Mom!" she said urgently. "What if Charity finds the way back here on her own, after we've moved? She won't know where we are, will she? We *have* to stay here until she's found. We've just got to!"

"Don't worry, dear. I'm sure she'll turn up before Wednesday," Mrs. Grace said, putting an arm around Josie's shoulder. "There are so many people out looking by now, and I don't think Kirsty will have gone too far away."

Josie passed a miserable afternoon, wandering among the half-packed trunks and boxes that filled the house and listening out for the phone. The only person who called was Anna, asking if she could come to stay the night at School Farm. Josie said yes at once, glad for some company to take her mind off things. She couldn't believe that Kirsty and Charity would be spending another night out in the open. Surely they should have been found by now? But by the time it was getting dark, and she and Anna were getting ready for bed, there had still been no news.

"It was bad enough trying to get used to the idea of Charity being sold," Josie said, "but this is even worse! I keep imagining all the awful things that might be happening."

"I'm sure Kirsty will take care of her," Anna said comfortingly. "She knows how to, doesn't she?"

"She might be able to ride okay, but she hasn't learned much about looking after a horse," Josie worried. "What if she does something stupid, like tying Charity up by her reins so that she hurts her mouth? Or she might let her drink when she's hot and blowing, and then she'll get colic. I can't bear to think about it, Anna!"

"Then don't think about it," Anna said sensibly, giving Josie a quick hug. "You'll only get more upset and that won't help anybody. Let's try and go to sleep. By the time it's morning, they'll probably have turned up somewhere, safe and well."

"Oh, I hope so," Josie sighed, taking one last look out of her bedroom window at the empty field before drawing the curtains. "I don't know what I'll do if anything happens to Charity!"

CHAPTER EIGHT

Josie found it almost impossible to sleep that night. She lay tossing and turning until it was almost light, listening to Anna's quiet breathing from the mattress on the floor next to her bed. Birds had begun to sing the dawn chorus by the time she eventually dropped off, and she didn't wake up until late morning. When she opened her bleary eyes, she saw that the mattress was empty. Anna was already down in the kitchen, sitting at the table with her mother and Ben and Mrs. Grace. One look at their tense faces told Josie there had been no news of Kirsty or Charity.

"Morning, sweetheart," her mother said, giving Josie a peck on the cheek. "We still haven't heard anything, I'm afraid. Dad's gone into school for his meeting, and I have to go to the police station to give a statement and answer some questions."

"Questions?" Josie asked, after she'd greeted everyone. She poured herself some orange juice, wishing her heavy, aching head would clear. "What kind of questions?"

"Oh, the kind of state I thought Kirsty was in when she left here, where she might have gone, that sort of thing," said Mrs. Grace, looking for her car keys on the table.

"I'll be staying here for a while this morning," Lynne added. "Just to keep an eye on things and listen for the phone in case there's any news. Ben's come up to lend a hand, too."

"I've got to go now," Mrs. Grace said, waving good-bye as she rushed out of the door. "I'll see you in a couple of hours, I hope. Be good!"

"So, are you guys going out on bikes again today?" Lynne asked, after they'd heard the front door slam. "I brought Ben's and Anna's bicycles in the van, just in case. And at least it's not raining anymore."

"I don't know," Anna sighed. "It's useless trying to cover the fields on bikes, and I'm sure that's where we should be looking."

"If only Tubber were still here," Ben put in, "I could have gone out on him. That would have been the best thing. We really need a horse to go across country."

"Too bad Hope's so far away," Lynne said thoughtfully. "I'm sure Liz wouldn't have minded you taking her away from Friendship House for the day."

"But Faith is much nearer!" Anna suddenly exclaimed. "I've just had a brain flash! We could give Jill and her mother a call and tell them what's happened. I'm sure they wouldn't mind lending Faith to us—not in these circumstances! Don't you think, Josie?"

"Maybe," Josie said, not wanting to land herself in one of Anna's impetuous schemes without thinking it through. "It *would* make it easier to look for Kirsty, that's for sure. But could Faith manage a long ride? And how would the Atterburys get her here? They don't live that close by."

"They've got a trailer, haven't they?" Anna said, all fired up and eager. "They might bring her over for us. Oh, come on, you guys. It's worth a try!"

"I suppose it wouldn't hurt to give them a call,"

Josie said. "They can always say no. What do you think, Lynne?"

"The main thing I'm concerned about is not giving your mother any more reason to worry," Lynne Marshall said, running a hand through her spiky blond hair and making the silver bracelets on her wrist jangle together. Ben and Anna had inherited their father's dark coloring, passed down from his Spanish mother, and no one would ever have guessed they were related to Lynne.

"What if you have an accident or something, Josie?" she went on. "You'd probably be the one riding Faith, wouldn't you?"

"I'm not sure. We haven't really decided about that," Josie said, but Ben and Anna were already nodding in agreement.

"Charity's really your horse," Anna said. "And I'm sure Kirsty would much rather see you than either of us, if you did find her."

"We'd have to decide on a route first," Josie said, beginning to catch some of Anna's enthusiasm. "Then you'd know where I was. We could figure out where Kirsty most likely would have gone, and I'll just cover as much ground as I can, depending on how Faith gets on. Oh, Anna, this could be the best idea you've ever had!"

"Look, Josie, I just have to be extra careful because your mom's not here," Lynne said. "I know she lets you go out riding on your own, but if anything happens, I'd be the one responsible." She dug in her huge leather shoulder bag and brought out a cell phone. "Here, take this with you," she said. "We'll stay back at base, and you can call us if you find anything or you need help."

"Oh, Mom, that's great!" Anna said, flinging her arms around her.

"Now, don't get carried away," Lynne laughed, disentangling herself. "You've still got to call the Atterburys, remember? And if they say no, you've got to accept their decision."

"Okay," Josie answered, rushing out to the hall to look for the address book and start phoning. *Oh, please say yes,* she prayed as she dialed the Atterburys' number. *This is such a good plan. It has to work!*

Jill answered the phone. She had already heard from friends who lived in Northgate that Kirsty and Charity were missing, and she was happy to help in any way she could. "Of course you can take Faith!" she told Josie. "It's a great idea, and it's nice to think of her looking for Charity. After all, she's kind of like her aunt, isn't she? I'll have to check with Mom first, though. We'll call you back in five minutes."

It seemed like an hour before the phone rang again, and Josie heard Mrs. Atterbury's voice on the other end of the line. "We'll be over in about half an hour," she said. "Jill's going to help me load Faith into the trailer, and we'll come as quickly as we can."

"Oh, thank you!" Josie said for the third time. "It's so kind of you—it really is!"

"Don't think anything of it," Mrs. Atterbury replied kindly. "We're just happy to be able to help. It's awful to think of that poor girl out on her own somewhere."

"Yes!" Josie called to the others, hurrying back into the kitchen. "Faith will be here in half an hour or so!"

"Then have some breakfast," Lynne said, pushing a bowl and a box of cereal across the table to her. "We don't want you fainting with hunger."

"What is it with mothers and this thing they have about breakfast?" Josie grumbled good-naturedly.

She suddenly felt wide awake and much too excited to eat anything.

"Here they are!" Anna called from the path outside School Farm, as a car towing a horse trailer pulled slowly into the Graces' yard.

"I think that's everything," Lynne said, tightening the drawstring of a small backpack and handing it to Josie in the hall. "The phone's in there, plus a flashlight I managed to find in one of those boxes in the kitchen. And there's a bag of horse treats, peppermints, granola bars, and a drink. You probably won't need any of it, but it's just as well to be prepared."

"Thanks, Lynne," Josie said, giving her a hug. "You've been great!"

She rushed out into the yard, to see Mrs. Atterbury beginning to unfasten the side ramp at the front of the trailer. Jill soon emerged, grinning from ear to ear and leading Faith slowly down the ramp. Josie felt a pang when she saw the elderly bay mare back in the yard where she'd spent so much of her life. She rushed over to greet the Atterburys and give Faith a cuddle.

"So how's my sweetheart?" she said, laying her head against the horse's smooth neck and feeling Faith nuzzle her hair. "She's looking even better than the last time I saw her," she added to Jill, patting Faith's glossy coat. "Do you think she's up for this, though?"

"You'll have to see how it goes," Jill said, "but I don't see why not. My friend Bev took her out quite a lot last week, so I think she's fit."

"I'm just so grateful to both of you," Josie said again as Mrs. Atterbury came over to join them. "At least now we feel like we're doing something."

"I told you, we're glad to help," Jill's mother replied. "And you and Faith must be the perfect team to go out looking for Charity."

"Come on," Anna said, beginning to unbuckle Faith's traveling boots. "Time you got a move on."

Soon Faith was tacked up, and Josie was fastening her riding helmet. Lynne and Mrs. Atterbury talked quietly together by the trailer while Ben, Anna, and Jill stood around the mounting block. "Do you really think this is going to do any good?" Josie asked them, suddenly suffering a last-minute attack of doubt now she was finally about to set off. "I mean, think of all the police out searching already. If they haven't found them, do you think I've got much chance?"

"Yes," Ben said firmly, holding on to the offside stirrup as Josie pulled herself up into the saddle. "You've got one big advantage—you know Kirsty. Try to put yourself in her shoes. Where would you have gone, if you were her? That's what we've tried to work out, isn't it?"

The three of them had thought back over all the times Kirsty had gone out riding, and which routes she had taken. "The woods it is, then," Josie said, shortening her reins. There was a wooded area at the top of a hill on one of their favorite rides. It was full of dens and natural shelters, formed by the thickly growing trees, and they'd decided there was a good chance Kirsty might have gone there. "If there's no sign of them, I'll follow Mom's path along the river and search the fields that way," Josie went on. "Anyway, I'll keep in touch by phone."

"I feel jealous now," Anna said enviously, rubbing Faith's nose. "It must feel great to be doing something constructive instead of just sitting here, waiting."

"Yes, it does," Josie admitted, surprised how much her spirits had risen. "It's great to be riding Faith again, for one thing. If we were just out for a ride, it would be perfect."

"Well, keep that for next time," Jill added. "Be careful, though, won't you? We can't imagine life without Faith now."

"Don't worry," Josie called as she rode out of the yard. "We'll be back safe and sound!" And maybe Charity will be with us, she couldn't help adding to herself.

"Come on, now, Faith," Josie said as they trotted up the hill to the woods. "We've got a job to do!" Kirsty had often ridden Charity this way before. Mrs. Grace would take her students up the hill, through the woods, and then down to the river and back across the fields. It made a perfect hourlong ride.

Josie shivered as she peered into the trees on either side of the narrow path, wondering how Kirsty had spent her second night out in the open. *Please let them both be safe and well*, she prayed to herself. *And please let me find them.*

"Kirsty! Charity!" she called softly, wondering

whether Kirsty wanted to be found by now,
or whether she'd try to run if she saw someone
coming. There was no reply—only a flurry of wings
as a couple of startled pigeons flew up from the
undergrowth. Josie could tell there was no one in the
woods but herself.

She reined Faith to a halt in the lane beyond the
woods, and reached for the cell phone in her
backpack on her back. "No sign of her in the
woods," she told Lynne. "I'll try down by the river."

"How's Faith doing?" Lynne asked. "Jill wants to
know how she is."

"Oh, fine," Josie said affectionately, giving the
horse's withers a scratch. "It's funny, but I think she
can tell something's up. She seems to know we're
not out here just for fun." It was true—Faith had
been walking along alertly, her head held high and
her ears flicking back and forth. Maybe some of the
urgency Josie felt was being transmitted to her.

"You'd like to go down by the river, wouldn't
you, Faith?" Josie said as they set off again, this time
along the bridle path. She looked around constantly,
straining to catch a glimpse of anything unusual, but
was always disappointed. Except for a couple of

police cars that passed her in the lane, everything was quiet. There had been several officers in the village, and even more with tracker dogs searching the fields immediately around it, but no one seemed to be looking out this way.

Josie rode Faith down through the wetlands until they reached the river, and then tried to turn her left, following the route Mrs. Grace usually took with her students. To her surprise, though, Faith wouldn't move. She planted her feet firmly on the ground and stood there, throwing her head up in the air and swishing her tail as Josie pulled on the left rein.

"Faith!" Josie said, astonished. "What are you doing?" She simply couldn't understand it. Faith had never been a naughty horse. She'd always done as she was told. What on earth was she behaving like this for? She kicked more firmly with her right leg, but Faith still wouldn't move. She threw up her head again and then took off to the right, so suddenly that Josie nearly fell off, trotting quickly along the river path in the other direction.

Josie's first instinct was to try to make Faith turn back the way she'd first asked her to go, but something about the horse's sense of purpose made her think again. There was an urgency in her pace that reminded Josie of Basil when he had caught the scent of a rabbit.

"Oh, well," she said to Faith, "you've got as much chance of finding them as I have, I suppose." She was puzzled, though—this stretch of the river took them past the boathouse and, as far as she knew, Kirsty had never come this way.

And yet . . . the boathouse! Wouldn't that be the perfect place to come if you needed somewhere to hide? It was secluded, for one thing—hardly anyone knew where it was or walked along that stretch of the river. The building was half falling down, but it would offer some shelter from the rain and wind, and no one could see into it from the river. The more Josie thought, the more convinced she became that the boathouse was definitely worth a look.

"Oh, well done, Faith!" she said, stroking her satiny neck. "You are a clever old thing!" The horse blew down her nose and trotted even faster, and, before Josie knew it, they were cantering along the path. She laughed, and let Faith take the lead.

Before long, the boathouse had come into sight, and Josie felt her heart lurch as she caught sight of its rotting timbers. Could Kirsty and Charity really be hiding there? It was such a forbidding, desolate place. Faith slowed to a bumpy trot and then a walk. Josie gave her a pat as they approached, to comfort herself with the feel of the horse's warm, smooth skin as much as anything.

There were no clues to be seen from the outside. Josie slipped her feet out of the stirrups and lightly jumped down. Quickly, she took off Faith's bridle, slipped on the head collar, and tied her to a fence post by the side of the path. "I won't be long," she said quietly. Then she stealthily approached the building for a closer look. The door was propped half open, revealing a glimpse of the dark rooms inside. Josie shivered, not exactly eager to venture in, and decided to take a proper look around the outside to see if there was any sign of life.

Faith seemed to be watching Josie anxiously as she crept around to the ruined side of the building. Being careful where she put her feet, she made her way cautiously toward the open courtyard. And there, tied to a window frame in the far corner, was Charity.

CHAPTER NINE

"Charity!" Josie shouted, quite forgetting to be quiet and rushing over to fling her arms round the horse's neck. "You're here! I've found you!" She smothered her with kisses, while Charity pushed her head into Josie's shoulder and neighed in welcome. Drawing back, Josie looked her quickly over to see what kind of state she was in. Her coat was dirty, but her eyes were bright and she seemed to be in fairly good shape. She was wearing a head collar, and her saddle and bridle were tucked in a sheltered corner near by.

"Oh, thank goodness," Josie sighed, laying her head against Charity's neck. The two of them stood quietly together for a moment, then Josie took off her backpack and began to search for the horse treats. "Here you are, girl. This'll keep you going for a bit," she said, holding a handful out flat on her palm. "We'll soon have you home!" Charity blew down her nose and crunched them up eagerly.

"Now for Kirsty," Josie said, turning to look at the other half of the boathouse. "She must be in there somewhere!"

Leaving Charity tied to the wall, she went back around to the front and peered through the open doorway. "Kirsty!" she called softly. "I know you're here. It's me, Josie! Don't be afraid."

But there was no reply. Summoning up her courage, Josie walked over the uneven threshold, around the half-open door, and into the room. She'd never been frightened when she'd come here with Anna and Ben, but this time things were different. She was all on her own, and she had no idea what she'd find. Kirsty might be hurt, and she would certainly be scared and upset.

Josie stared around the room, but she could tell at a glance it was empty. There were no possible hiding places. "Kirsty," she called again nervously, walking on toward the doorway into the back room. "Don't worry! I've come to help you."

This door was shut. There was nothing Josie would have rather done than simply walk away from it and take Charity home, but she knew she had to go on. Kirsty might be on the other side of the door, and she might be in trouble. Telling herself to be brave, Josie pushed the door open, her heart thumping. This room, too, was bare. There was no sign of life—only the bench, and the rotting life jacket underneath it, met her gaze. Beside the life jacket, however, was a strange-looking blue plastic object. Josie walked over and picked it up, trying to work out what on earth it could be. And then she remembered where she'd seen something similar. A boy at her school had once had an asthma attack after gym, and he'd used one of these to help him breathe. It was an inhaler. Kirsty's inhaler. It must be! So where was she?

Josie stared out of the window above the bench, hardly daring to imagine what she might find. She caught a flurry of movement out of the corner of one eye—a wisp of blond hair and a flash of pale skin. Her heart began to pound wildly as she rushed toward the door leading out to the veranda. Kirsty wouldn't have gone out there, would she have? It was so unsafe! She couldn't be so stupid!

But she had. Josie couldn't believe her eyes as she looked through the big hole in the door frame where once there had been glass. There was Kirsty, huddled against the wooden railings of the veranda and staring back at her with terrified eyes.

"Don't worry, Kirsty!" Josie called in a shaking voice. "It's only me. I won't hurt you!"

"Don't come out here!" Kirsty cried. "Leave me alone!" She was obviously frightened out of her wits.

Josie tried to think of what she could say to reassure her. She cleared her throat and licked her dry lips. "But I can't leave you here, Kirsty," she said soothingly. "Why don't we go home together? Faith's here. I've tied her up outside. You can ride Charity back, if you like."

Kirsty didn't reply. Slowly, Josie began to push the door further open. "No one's angry at you," she went on. "We're all just very worried. Your mom's desperate to know where you are."

Kirsty's lower lip began to tremble, and Josie could see she was close to tears. Poor thing, she thought to herself. She's backed herself into a corner and she doesn't know how to get out of it. "You've looked after Charity very well," she said gently. "But now it's time to take her home."

"I didn't mean to upset anyone," Kirsty gasped, the tears beginning to spill over on to her cheeks.

"It doesn't matter now," Josie said. She gave the door a final push and prepared to step out on to the veranda, but when she looked down at it, her blood froze. The whole thing was even more unstable than she'd first thought. There were huge gaps in the rotten floorboards, and the rickety structure was swaying alarmingly. If she put her full weight on it, too, the veranda would almost certainly collapse. Kirsty would have to get off it on her own.

"Come over to me, Kirsty," she said. "But you'll have to move very slowly. Do you understand? Take it gently—no sudden movements."

Kirsty looked around as though she had absolutely no idea where she was. She must have rushed out to the veranda without thinking, in her anxiety to hide. When she saw the danger she was in, her eyes widened at once and she dropped to a sitting position.

"It's all right," Josie said as calmly as she could, though the sight of the veranda shaking as Kirsty moved terrified her. "You can shuffle over on your bottom, if you like. Just come to me." And she stretched out her arms.

"Josie! I'm scared," Kirsty said in a quavering voice. There was a tight, wheezing sound coming from her chest as she spoke, and she seemed to be having trouble breathing.

"Don't worry, Kirsty. You'll be fine," Josie replied, trying not to show her own fear. "Come on—it's not far!"

Kirsty just shook her head, though. She had gone as white as a sheet, and her eyes were fixed and staring. "Can't . . . breathe!" she said painfully, her arms wrapped around her chest.

Josie's mind raced. Then she remembered what she was still holding tightly in her sweating hand. "Look, I've got your inhaler," she said. "I'll throw it across to you. When it lands, don't grab it—just reach for it very slowly. Okay?"

Kirsty nodded, her eyes still locked on to Josie's. "Here it comes," Josie said, her heart in her mouth. Carefully, she took aim and lobbed the inhaler so that it landed about two feet from Kirsty's hand. Just a little too short.

"Reach for it slowly, remember," Josie said, trying not to show her concern. "No sudden movements."

Kirsty nodded and shuffled a little way forward. The veranda lurched. She stretched out a trembling hand and took her gaze away from Josie just long enough to grab the inhaler and put it into her mouth. The look of panic left her eyes and her shoulders relaxed as she breathed in the medication.

"That's better, isn't it?" Josie said, forcing herself to smile. "Now let's get you off this veranda. Stay sitting down, and come toward me. That's the way!" As soon as she's inside, I can call for help, she decided to herself. She felt that if she took her eyes off Kirsty for a second, the terrified girl would lose her head completely.

Inch by agonizing inch, Kirsty struggled closer. Josie's nails were digging into her palms, and her jaw was aching with the effort of smiling. And then, suddenly, the inhaler slipped out of Kirsty's grasp.

"No!" she cried, leaning quickly forward to grab for it. With a terrible, bloodcurdling crash, the rotted wood on which she was sitting gave way, and she plunged through the floor.

"Josie! Help me!" she screamed, desperately

clinging on to the edge of the gaping hole. Her head and shoulders were visible, and her arms scrabbling at the splintering wood, but the rest of her must have been hanging in midair above the swirling river.

"I'm coming!" Josie cried. There was no time to think. Quickly, she threw off the backpack and, dropping to her knees, stretched full length on her stomach across the unstable veranda floor. "Take my hand!" she shouted urgently.

"I can't!" Kirsty shouted, desperately trying to reach Josie's outstretched fingers. "I'm slipping!"

Another section of wood began to crack as Kirsty struggled to hold on. Despite all her desperate efforts, however, she began to slide farther down. And after seconds which seemed to last hours, she finally lost her grip and vanished from sight.

There was a scream, a splash . . . and then, nothing.

Josie could tell the whole veranda was about to give way at any moment. Quickly, she wriggled back on her stomach to the door as several more floorboards fell away, and dived inside the boathouse. She rushed over to the window. At first, she couldn't see anything in the river below, but then she suddenly caught sight of Kirsty's blond hair swirling out in a cloud on the water. She had managed to catch hold of an upright post with an anchor attached to it.

"Help!" Kirsty screamed. There was a very strong current in the river at this point, and she was fighting to hold on to the anchor.

"Hang on!" Josie shouted. She picked up the life jacket to throw it out of the window, but the crumbling material fell to pieces in her hands. Her heart thumping, she rushed out of the boathouse and threw herself down the bank to reach the river's edge. She waded into the water, hardly noticing how cold it was. "I'm coming!" she shouted again to Kirsty as she struggled out toward her.

But Josie found it almost impossible to make any headway at all. The current was against her, and every step forward was a huge effort. Trying to swim was no better, and she felt herself powerless against the force of the river. She was now out of her depth and quickly becoming exhausted. Kirsty wasn't very far out, but there seemed no way she could reach her. At this rate, they would both drown.

And then, suddenly, Josie heard another splash.

Turning around, she saw a flash of white and realized, to her amazement, that Charity was swimming toward her. The horse's eyes were rolling as she struggled to keep her head above water, while, beneath the surface, she threw out her long legs steadily.

"Charity!" Josie exclaimed. She couldn't believe that her wonderful horse had managed to free herself and come out to rescue them, but here she was. And in the nick of time, too. Josie sobbed with relief as Charity swam nearer, and she felt her solid, reassuring presence next to her in the river. She flung out one arm and grasped a handful of her mane, feeling the current force her back against Charity's strong neck. And then she caught sight of the nylon lead rope, trailing out from her head collar. If they could just swim out a little farther, maybe she could throw it to Kirsty.

"Kirsty! Charity's here!" she called over. "She's come to help us." She saw to her alarm that Kirsty was tiring, too. She only just managed to turn her head in their direction.

"Come on, Charity!" Josie urged. "You can do it." The horse's breath was coming in great gasps as she struggled with all her strength against the surging water. Slowly but surely, though, they were moving forward. Seconds later, Josie judged they were near enough for the rope to be within Kirsty's grasp.

"Catch this!" she shouted loudly, and hurled the end of the lead rope toward her. It floated close by, but Kirsty was obviously terrified of letting go of the post and being carried off by the current.

"Take it!" Josie screamed, hanging on to Charity's head collar to keep herself afloat. "It's your only chance!"

With one last look at Charity, Kirsty seemed to summon up all her courage. Still holding on to the anchor, she managed to grab the rope with one hand. Then, closing her eyes and gritting her teeth, she let go of the post altogether, launched herself into the water, and grasped the rope with both hands.

"Yes!" Josie shouted. "Now, hold on—we'll get you back."

Charity wheeled around, her legs thrashing, and swam strongly toward the riverbank. She seemed to know exactly what to do. It was much easier going back this way, since the current was behind them now. Anxiously, Josie looked back. Kirsty's head kept sinking under the water, but she was still hanging on to the strong nylon rope with all her might.

Soon Josie could feel solid ground beneath her feet, and, a few seconds later, she was able to put her arms around Kirsty and lift up her head. Coughing and spluttering, they staggered out of the water together and collapsed on the riverbank.

"Charity saved me," Kirsty gasped, when she was able to speak.

"Yes," Josie answered as she got her breath back. Her heart overflowed with love and pride as she looked at the exhausted horse standing on the bank next to them. "Sweet Charity. She saved us both."

CHAPTER TEN

"Will you be okay if I go to the boathouse?" Josie asked Kirsty, as they tried to recover, sitting on the grass. "I left my bag there, and the cell phone's inside it."

Kirsty nodded, so Josie staggered to her feet and went off to call for help. Charity was obviously tired—Josie could see that as she went past—but she was up on her feet. And at least now they weren't in any immediate danger.

Josie retrieved the backpack from the floor of the back room where she'd tossed it aside what seemed like hours earlier, and dug out the phone. Should she call the police straight away, or School Farm? Feeling a sudden need to talk to her parents, she decided to phone home. "Mom! I've found Charity, and Kirsty, too," she said breathlessly, so relieved to hear her mother's voice on the line that her legs suddenly weakened underneath her.

"How are they? Is everything okay? Where are you?" Mrs. Grace replied urgently.

Josie slid into a sitting position against the wall. "We're at the boathouse," she said. "We're all right, but I think Kirsty needs to see a doctor quickly. She's lost her inhaler and I'm worried she's going to have an asthma attack. We're both soaking wet."

"Soaking wet?" Mrs. Grace repeated. "What on earth have you been doing?"

"I'll explain later," Josie replied wearily. "Please, Mom, can you get help as soon as possible?"

"Of course," Mrs. Grace replied crisply. "Just stay where you are. Got that? Don't move!"

Josie made her way back to where Kirsty was sitting on the riverbank. She flopped back down beside her and rummaged in the backpack for the granola bars and thermos. "Help yourself," she said, offering them to Kirsty. "I've called the stables. Someone will be coming to get us soon."

"My mother's going to be really angry with me,"

Kirsty said anxiously. She took a couple bites of the granola bar and washed them down with several mouthfuls from the thermos. "I'm sorry that I've caused everyone so much trouble."

"Oh, it's all right," Josie replied. "I bet your mother will be so happy to see you she won't be angry at all. But why did you do it, Kirsty? You couldn't have stayed out here forever."

"I know," Kirsty sighed. "I just couldn't let Charity be taken away from you and sold to some stranger. I thought if we hid for a while, your parents might change their minds and let you keep her."

"But they don't want to sell Charity any more than I do!" Josie said. "We've just got to. There's no way around it. And your stealing her wasn't ever going to make any difference."

"I wasn't stealing her!" Kirsty cried, looking horrified at the suggestion. "I was keeping her for you, Josie. I thought you'd be pleased with me!"

"Oh, Kirsty," Josie said, "that's not the way to go about things. Look at the trouble you got into! I'd never have come to the boathouse if it hadn't been for Faith, and you might not have been found."

"What do you mean?" Kirsty asked curiously.

"What did Faith have to do with it?"

"Well, somehow she knew where you and Charity were," Josie replied. "I only came out here because she wanted to come this way. It's such a dangerous place. What if you'd fallen into the water when no one was around? And we both probably would have drowned if it hadn't been for Charity."

"They've been amazing," Kirsty said, looking over to where the two horses were standing, peacefully grazing on the long grass at the edge of the path. Charity had caught sight of Faith, tied to the fence post, and trotted up to greet her with several nuzzles and playful nips.

"I don't understand how Charity managed to get out to us in the river, though," Kirsty went on. "I'm sure she was tied up properly. I used that special knot you showed me once."

"A quick release knot?" Josie asked, smiling. "Well, those are Charity's specialty. She pulls the loose end of the rope with her teeth, and the knot's undone in three seconds flat."

"I've never met a horse like her," Kirsty said. "Your parents just can't sell her now, Josie! Not after she saved us."

Josie lay back on the grass and closed her eyes, too tired to waste any more time trying to explain. Dimly she became aware of the sound of car engines, gradually growing louder. Sitting up, she and Kirsty saw two police cars bumping their way toward them over the uneven ground along the riverbank. When the path narrowed, they were forced to stop. The passenger door of the first car was flung open, and a woman came running over the grass. "Kirsty!" she shouted, tears streaming down her face. It was Mrs. Fisher, and Josie could see at once that Kirsty had nothing to worry about. She wasn't about to get scolded.

"You were so brave!" Anna said admiringly. She was sitting at the end of the sofa at Josie's feet, listening to the whole story all over again. Lynne and Ben had gone home, but Anna couldn't tear herself away. "Wasn't it incredible that Faith knew where they were?" she added. "And that Charity went into the river after you?"

Josie nodded. "I wouldn't be here now if it weren't for her," she said.

"Charity seems to be fine," Mr. Grace

announced, coming into the sitting room with some cartons of juice and a plate of sandwiches. "Mom's given her a hot bran mash, and she's turning in."

Kirsty had been taken to the hospital with her mother for a thorough examination. Mary Grace had come in the second police car with Ben and Anna, so Josie was taken back home by car with her mother, wrapped in a blanket. The twins had ridden the horses back to School Farm, where the Atterburys were waiting to take Faith home in the trailer. Charity was now recovering in her stall.

"I suppose we'd better tell the Taylors she's here," Josie said, leaning back against the cushions. "They're meant to be picking her up tomorrow, aren't they?" She didn't want to think about how painful that was going to be. Still, at least now she knew Charity was safe and well.

"Well," Mr. Grace said, sitting on the edge of the sofa, "we've actually put the Taylors on hold for the moment."

"On hold?" Josie repeated, looking at her father curiously. "What do you mean?"

"I think I've found somewhere that might suit Charity better," Mr. Grace replied. "Nothing's definite yet, but I've asked the Taylors to give us a little more time before they come for her."

"But you're moving the day after tomorrow, aren't you?" Anna said. "There isn't much time left!"

"And what is this place?" Josie asked. "I thought we'd agreed the Taylors could give her the best home we were going to get."

"Almost the best home," her father said mysteriously, getting up to leave the room—"but not quite."

"Dad!" Josie said indignantly. "Aren't you going to tell me any more than that?"

"There's not much more I can say at the moment," Mr. Grace replied. "Don't worry about anything, sweetheart. I'll let you know the minute it's all worked out."

Josie and Anna exchanged looks. "Well, something's going on, that's for sure!" Josie said. "Dad's still wearing a suit, for one thing, and I wonder why he had to go to that meeting this morning?"

"It gets stranger and stranger," Anna said. "I hate it when parents know something and you don't. Maybe you can try and get the information out of your mom."

"Yes, maybe," Josie replied. But when she cornered Mrs. Grace in the kitchen after Anna had gone home, her mother was just as tight-lipped.

"This is your father's idea," she said. "He hasn't told me the full story, either. He just keeps saying we've got to trust him and we'll find out everything tomorrow."

"But tomorrow we're moving!" Josie wailed. "This is all so last minute!"

"You're telling me!" her mother replied. "All this business with Kirsty has really set me back. I'm never going to get all the packing finished!"

"Have you heard how Kirsty is?" Josie asked.

"Yes, I called the hospital last night, when you'd gone to bed," Mrs. Grace replied. "They were just keeping her in overnight to be on the safe side, but she doesn't seem to have come to any harm."

"Good," Josie said. "I know Anna thinks I'm crazy, but I still can't help feeling a bit sorry for her. I wonder if the new owners would let her come and ride Charity sometimes?"

"Well, that would be up to them," her mother replied. "Whoever it is that ends up having Charity."

* * *

"So, have you got anywhere with solving the mystery?" Anna said as soon as she saw Josie the next day. She'd come up to share the last afternoon they would spend together at School Farm, and found Josie in Charity's stall.

"No, I haven't," Josie replied irritably. "Mom says Dad hasn't told her everything, but I'm sure she knows more than I do. Why won't they tell me what's going on? I've got a right to know, after all." She was trying to soothe her feelings by giving Charity a full groom but, so far, it wasn't working.

"Why don't we braid Charity's mane and tail?" Anna suggested. "That's the sort of job that'll take your mind off things, and she looks so beautiful when it's done. I'll do the mane—you know I'm hopeless with her tail."

"All right," Josie said, rather gracelessly. "Might as well, I suppose. It'll keep us out of the house. Dad's disappeared somewhere, as usual, and Mom keeps unpacking boxes and then packing them again. It's a nightmare."

For a while, they worked together quietly, not talking much. "I can't believe Charity's going to be sent off tomorrow, and we don't even know where,"

Anna said eventually. "After everything that's happened!"

"You're beginning to sound like Kirsty," Josie said. "I told her, what Charity did yesterday doesn't make any difference to the fact that we haven't got enough money to keep her."

"It's so sad," Anna sighed as she snapped an elastic band around one sleek white braid. "You know, this morning I called the real-estate agent and found out who owns that field behind the house. It belongs to a local farmer. I called him at lunchtime but he says someone else has asked him to keep a space for a horse in the field, so he wouldn't have room for Charity, anyway."

"Well, it was nice of you to try," Josie said resignedly. "We couldn't have afforded it, though. I'm afraid it's too late to try and change things, Anna."

Charity spent her last night at School Farm in the stall, so the Graces didn't have to worry about catching her in the morning. Josie was up and dressed the next day before either of her parents. There was a terrible sinking feeling in the pit of her stomach as she watched her father eat his way through a mountain of toast, then wash the plate and pack it with the others in the trunk. He seemed to be quite unconcerned. When Josie caught his eye, he even smiled at her. How could he?

"Oh, the mail should have arrived by now," he said, looking at his watch. "Just think, it's the last delivery we'll have here. Josie, will you go and check the mailbox?"

"Okay," she replied, glad of something to do. Basil followed her as she wandered out of the house, through the yard, and down the drive. All the commotion was making him nervous, and he obviously felt he couldn't let anyone out of his sight for a second, in case he was left behind. She opened the rusty mailbox flap and took out a horse feed catalog for her mother and a letter for her father.

"That's the one!" he said when she brought it back, tearing the envelope open. "Great! I've been waiting for this." And he read the letter with a look of deep satisfaction that made Josie feel even more irritated.

"Just a couple of phone calls to make before we're off," he said when he'd finished, rubbing his hands and hurrying out of the kitchen. "Mary! Where are you? I need to talk to you!"

Fifteen minutes later, he was back. "Okay, Josie," he said. "If you and your mother could just load Charity into the trailer, we can take her off to her new home. We'd better bring her tack, too."

"Dad!" Josie burst out. "You've got to tell me where you're taking her. Why are you being so secretive?"

"Don't worry, sweetheart," he replied. "You'll know everything soon. I want you to come with me. I'd rather not have to unload Charity on my own, and Mom has to stay here for the moving men."

"Oh," Josie said, taken aback. She didn't know if she was quite up to being there when Charity was handed over. It had been hard enough seeing Emily Taylor riding her. But, on the other hand, it seemed as if it was going to be the only way she was going to find out more about this new home.

"Go on, Josie," her mother said, appearing in the kitchen with the vacuum cleaner in one hand and a black trash bag in the other. "It's not far, and Dad needs you with him."

"Okay," Josie said. So this was it. She'd just have

to prepare herself for the worst.

She put on Charity's traveling boots and her tail guard, then led her out of her stall for the last time and up the ramp into the trailer. "Say good-bye to School Farm, Charity," Robert Grace said cheerfully, fastening the bolts behind her. Josie shot him a suspicious look, but there was obviously no point in asking any more questions. She would have to wait to find out.

They drove through the town of Littlehaven and continued along the main road out of it. "We'll be coming to Lime Tree Lodge in a minute," Josie remarked, feeling somehow consoled by the thought. Maybe Charity wouldn't be too far away, and she could go and visit her sometimes.

"Yes, we will, and as it happens I just have to make a stop there quickly," Mr. Grace replied. Soon he was turning off the main road and driving through the big iron gates. But he went on past the cottage and started up another long drive. He pulled in opposite the gate that belonged to the field that backed on to Lime Tree Lodge.

"Why have you stopped here?" Josie asked, as her father turned off the engine.

"So we can settle Charity in her new home," he said. "What are you sitting there for, Josie? I told you, I can't manage on my own."

"But—but I can't believe it!" Josie stammered. "This is *our* new home! What are you saying? Come on, Dad, put me out of my misery!"

"I'm saying," he answered, grinning from ear to ear, "that you can keep her!"

Josie launched herself across the seat to give her father a big hug. "But I still don't understand!"

"Well," said Mr. Grace, disentangling himself from Josie's grip. "I called the Taylors this morning to let them know that our circumstances have changed. And to apologize. They were really nice about it, though."

"But how have our circumstances changed?" Josie said. She couldn't believe what she was hearing. Such wonderful, incredible, fantastic news would take time to sink in.

"Because your father is now head of the English and Drama Department at Littlehaven High," Mr. Grace answered, looking very pleased with himself. "That's what my letter confirmed this morning. I didn't want to say anything until I knew for certain.

The job suddenly became vacant because my colleague who's been doing it for years announced he was moving away. The headmaster wanted to appoint a replacement before September, so I had an interview on Monday. I got the job, and quite a lot more money to go with it!"

"Oh, Dad!" Josie said, hugging him even more tightly. "That's fantastic! Thank you so, so much. Our new home is going to be just perfect now that Charity can share it with us!" And then she couldn't say any more, because all the excitement and fear and suspense of the last few months and days were dissolving in a great wave of happiness.

"Come on, Josie," her father said gently. "Let's get this horse into the field before she thinks we've forgotten about her."

"Okay!" Josie replied, swallowing her tears of joy and relief. "My own sweet Charity. Now nothing's going to take her away from me!"